The Twenty Committee

Mark J. Whitney

Copyright © 2023 Mark J. Whitney
All rights reserved.
ISBN: 9798864557655

DEDICATION

In memory of my Mom, Diane Saborowski (nee Foerester) who passed away December 8, 2022. Mom was an avid reader and, I would like to think she would have enjoyed this story. Love you Mom.

ACKNOWLEDGMENTS

As always, I must first thank my wife, Joanne Brooks, for her unwavering support, her attention to detail in editing and, most of all, for putting up with me. I also need to thank my first readers, who never fail to help me flesh out my story. This is no small task, as my first draft is generally very thin. My step mother, Linda Whitney, my dear friends Linda Buchanan, Alex (Bo) McLean and his lovely wife Laurie, Maureen Burgess and my sister in law Peggy Brooks. This book isn't possible without your help.

PROLOGUE

I'm huddled in the cold dark with Oskar and Lucas. We are perched on the Hardanger Plateau in Norway high above the hydro plant we've been sent to destroy, my beard caked in ice and snow. We are all silent in our thoughts, praying that the explosives we've set will do the job. Noah and Isak have already left, on their way back to the village and (hopefully) a warm bed.

I find myself thinking of my family back home in Canada, and how I ended up here. Mostly, I think of my grandfather and how proud he would be if I was able to tell him what I was up to. But of course, that isn't possible, or allowed, given the secrecy of what we do.

My grandfather, Emil Andersen, emigrated from Norway to Canada as a young man in 1882. He settled near the town of Port Hope, Ontario, lured by the prospect of inexpensive land and a burgeoning lumber industry. A short two years later, after working long, laborious days, Emil had saved enough money to buy a small farm. He married my grandmother, another Norwegian immigrant, that same year and in 1884 my father was born.

It still saddens me to think of my father. I think of him often and am reminded of him whenever I look in a mirror. I look like a younger version; six two, one hundred and ninety pounds, average build with blue eyes and blond hair. My grandmother never tires of reminding me of this.

My grandmother practically raised me, especially in my younger years, since my mother died giving birth and my father was far too busy running the farm alongside my aging grandfather. Despite losing my mother I had a good childhood and excelled at school. In 1939 I graduated from Queen's University with an Engineering degree.

I will never forget my father's shock and dismay after the Nazis invaded Norway in 1940. Despite being born in Canada, he agreed wholeheartedly with my grandparents that the Nazis must be driven from their Norwegian homeland. I remember overhearing kitchen table discussions as my father wished to enlist, but he knew he was needed to farm the land.

Just weeks after the invasion, my father died in a tragic farm accident, after being severely lacerated by a grain auger. His last words to me were, "Marcus… promise me that you will take care of your Bestemor and Bestefar"; that is, my grandmother and grandfather.

After the funeral, I spoke to my grandfather of my father's last words, and my concerns about them running the farm without him. He looked at me like I was mad. He said in his harsh Norwegian, "Marcus... I'm not in need of a babysitter. For a man of 78 I am still in fine shape, as is your Bestemor. I only wish I could return to Norway and fight those Nazi pigs that have overrun our homeland. I know that if your father could, he'd be there to fight."

The next day, I walked into a recruitment office in Oshawa and enlisted. From there, the next three years have been chaotic, yet fulfilling.

I recall the day that my handler approached me. I had finished drilling with my regiment and was about to go to the mess hall for breakfast. I noticed a man who appeared as if by magic at the door to our barracks. He was ordinary in appearance. Neither slight nor heavyset, of medium height with no distinguishing facial features. His clothing was not military, plain and rather unremarkable. Nonetheless, I had the oddest feeling when I caught him looking at me. I sensed immediately that it was his plan for me to catch him observing me, and that he might at any moment disappear into the shadows. Had he not wanted me to notice him, there is no doubt in my mind that I would not have.

He tipped his hat and said in slightly accented Norwegian, "Marcus, jeg er din nye sjef, bli med meg", which I recognized as, 'Marcus, I am your new commanding officer, come with me.' And, so began my journey into the world of espionage as part of His Majesty's Secret Service.

He had an air about him. I did not question him, I simply did what I was told and followed him to the commissioned officers' quarters. There, in the office usually reserved for the camp commander, he proceeded to tell me that I had been selected for the secret service and what the next several months (and possibly years) would look like. He introduced himself as 'William' and that henceforth, I would refer to him only by his code name 'Intrepid'.

"First of all, and of primary importance, every utterance between you and myself will be top secret. If you are found to be guilty of breaking this trust, you will be dealt with in the harshest of manners. Is that understood?" It was a rhetorical question and by 'harshest' the look in his eyes made me think of only one thing: death. "You have been selected for this assignment for two reasons: one, you speak fluent Norwegian and, I'm given to understand, have a good understanding of their customs and culture; two: you are a Queen's Engineering graduate." I nodded my head, still not able to speak.

"I am here to collect you for your training, where you will be surrounded by Norwegian expats. All of you will be trained in covert operations. When you are ready, you will be parachuted behind enemy lines in Norway. At that time, you will make contact with locals who are already in touch with Home Office via encrypted radio transmissions. These locals will guide you to your objective, where you and your team will reconnoiter the target. Once you have determined how best to destroy the target, you will be supplied appropriately via your new friends in the underground, and will complete your mission."

That was almost three years ago. As I think now about that conversation it is staggering to me how perfectly orchestrated it all seemed. Intrepid was almost prescient in explaining to me exactly how everything for my mission would unfold. Of course, I later learned that two previous missions had failed. Was I fortunate, or had those poor souls paved the way for my success? I liked to think our preparation was the ultimate factor.

It took eighteen months for me to train with my team. I had to immerse myself in Norwegian language, customs and cultures so that, once behind enemy lines, I could blend in seamlessly with the locals. I spent time at Camp X, located not far from Port Hope near the town of Whitby on the north shore of Lake Ontario, learning spy craft and sabotage techniques. At night I spent my time in the Little Norway neighbourhood in Toronto, about 40 miles west of Whitby. Going back and forth by rail as a real estate developer was my cover.

Little Norway was a perfect training ground. A community of roughly 3,500 souls, it was an oasis of expat Norwegians who had fled from Nazi terror. I was billeted on the outskirts of Little Norway and it was an easy walk to the local restaurants and taverns that sprang up in the new community. There I befriended many of these brave men and women who had left their homeland and had not surrendered by succumbing to despair. All were convinced that one day they would return and avenge. I was invited into their homes and treated to traditional Norwegian meals (many that my grandmother had already introduced me to). I attended Lutheran church services in the Nordic language. I went to weddings, communions, funerals. In short, I became as much Norwegian as my grandparents.

At Camp X in Whitby, I learned how to kill men with any and all weapons, including my bare hands. More importantly, I learned how to avoid having to do that. Killing was a last resort. To be a successful spy, the objective is to avoid bringing attention to yourself. Leaving a trail of bodies does not help in that regard. Nonetheless, one must be prepared, and now I know that to be all too true.

The vast majority of my Camp X training was in the art of sabotage. This is where my education as an engineer put me at an advantage, and was the primary reason I was selected to be the leader of our small cell of saboteurs. The most obvious objective of the saboteur is to destroy the target without inadvertently killing yourself, members of your team, or civilians. However, a truly gifted saboteur will also know how to destroy the target using the least amount of resources, and hopefully also inflict significant collateral damage on the enemy.

Finally, a saboteur who is also a spy must also

know how to elude capture. I wholeheartedly embraced that concept. Covering your tracks was grilled into me. But the final stage of training at Camp X was the most harrowing. The focus of that training was what to do in the unfortunate event that you are taken alive by the enemy. Most of my colleagues did not experience the rigour in training that I did in this regard because, other than myself, none were in contact with Home Office or any members of the Norwegian resistance leaders. This isolation of duties was done for their safety but also in the interest of security. While this training focused on how to resist and manipulate an interrogation, as a finale, I was also instructed on how to quickly kill myself should my interrogators prove to be too persistent. I carry my cyanide capsule at all times. A quick pop in the mouth, a jab with the molars and I'm off to oblivion, my interrogators left with misinformation to sift through and a body to dispose of.

As I think of it now I shiver. Of course, shivering is all we are doing tonight as Lucas, Oskar and I wait patiently for the detonation. Finally, as our timers reach the appointed time, the night sky lights up and a thunderous roar is heard far down the slope. Three separate charges explode in quick succession. As we observe from our plateau vantage point, orange, red, and yellow colours light up the sky, then white and dark gray smoke billow overhead. It's like a magnificent New Year's fireworks celebration, reminding me of the displays I've seen over the expanse of Lake Ontario; the only thing missing are the cheers of the spectators.

After the explosions, there is an almost eerie silence. The Vemork power station at the Rjukan waterfall is in ruins, as the clouds of smoke and dust waft upwards to our plateau like the cumulous clouds that adorn the Sistine Chapel. Only when the Germans sound the alarm and we hear the shrill voices of panicked officers do we silently nod at each other with satisfaction and begin our retreat. Lucas and Oskar do not know it yet, but we are to rendezvous with Royal Marines in the fjord about ten miles northwest of our current position. There, we will be rowed out to an awaiting submarine and transported back to England.

Three years of my life in His Majesty's Service have culminated in this moment. I have feelings of immense pride and relief, but I cannot also help but ponder the future. A future that I know all too well could be very grim. You see, as Intrepid noted when he first recruited me, I am an engineer. And, although Intrepid did not tell me why we were sent to blow up this power station in the middle of nowhere, I know enough to understand its significance. Being trained as a spy, one cannot help but ask questions. And through a porous network of locals who work at the plant and enjoy talking about their work over beers at the local watering holes, applying my Sherlock Holmes skill set I was able to figure out that the Vemork power station is the Nazi source for heavy water. Actually, Holmes would have laughed, I was more like Watson. And, given that my engineering training had also touched on theories behind the emerging technology of atomic energy, I understand exactly what the Nazis were doing here. I feel like a jumble of mixed metaphors as an involuntary shudder makes its way down my spine, like a black cat walking across my grave.

"Sofia… listen to me. No matter what you hear, you mustn't come out of here. Do you understand?" She has been nervously peering out the window, and I can hear the clomping of heavy boots on the road outside of our house.

I nod solemnly. I so desperately want to disobey Mama -- after all, I'm not a little girl anymore. I'm a woman of twenty-three. But, I can tell she is very serious by the strain on her face, and I obey her as her little girl, not wanting to add to that despair. Her eyes, usually bright and framed with smile lines, are now pools of darkness, her forehead creased with anxiety. I have not seen her this way ever, although, since the Germans overran our city of Minsk, destroying eighty percent of the beautiful buildings in the process, she has certainly had little to smile about. They arrived in Minsk several months ago, and we have not seen or heard from my father, since. He vowed to join the resistance, and to return to us when it was safe.

Above my head, she closes the trap door leading to our cellar hideaway. I'm swallowed by darkness, as I gingerly feel my way down the steps, the ceiling at the bottom so low that I must crouch so I don't hit my head. I hear the table being set down over the throw rug that conceals the hatch door. I dare not light the lamp sitting down here for fear of a sliver of light shining through an unseen crack or the smell of kerosene giving me away.

Less than five minutes have passed. Suddenly I hear a crash and heavy footfalls above me, three, possibly four men. My mother, with a calmness that belies the turmoil she must surely be feeling, says, "What are you doing here? Why would you harass a poor old woman? Does the SS not have better things to do?"

The response is in broken Polish that I can barely make out, but the words are not important. Then menace they imply is universal. Then, my world crumbles. My mother shouts with disgust, then screams with horror and despair. I hear men's laughter. Brutal, repugnant laughter. Then my mother stops screaming, and I hear her now sobbing inconsolably.

The cruel laughter continues. I've lost track of time, and my mother is now silent. Suddenly I hear a shrill scream from one of her assailants.

"You bitch! You've stabbed me! Ernest, Hans… help, she stabbed me!"

The report of small gun fire is immediate. Two shots in quick succession.

"Let's get you back to headquarters, Heinrich. The doctor will patch you up. Leave the Jew bitch here to rot. Nobody will care that we killed the wife of that terrorist Novartov – he's dead now anyway."

The bile rises in my throat as I fight the urge to scramble out of the basement and save my mother. But, I know it's too late. She's dead.

Finally there is silence from above, and the recriminations come immediately. If only it was her down here instead of me. If only there was a third person that could have placed the rug and table over the trap door so we could be down here together. If only Papa was here to protect us. Papa! Did they say he was dead? I feel as if I want to die. If only Mama had listened to me when I begged her to leave with me and go east. Perhaps we would have found Papa. Perhaps we'd still be safe and all together.

Eventually my sobbing subsides. Enough. There is no time for recriminations, and I realize I am now completely alone... Mama and Papa both victims of the barbarian Nazis. I huddle in the darkness, my knees pressed against my chest. I don't know how long I sit like this, but, as my brain starts to process again, something odd happens.

No, it is no longer grief I am feeling, nor regrets for what might have been. What I feel is pure, unadulterated hate. Now is the time for revenge. I, Sofia Novartov, will find a way to hurt the Germans. I swear if it the last thing I do, I will have vengeance, no matter what it takes, so help me God.

I climb the stairs, and mustering all my strength I push the hatch to our hiding spot open, toppling the table in the process. I see my mother,

her dress pushed up, underwear torn and tossed on the floor. I see the blood matted in her hair and pooled on the floor around her head and beside her body. In her hand, I see the knife... the knife she used to stab one of her assailants. · She did this knowing she would die. She did this knowing that the swines who were raping her would scatter like cockroaches, and I would be safe. I feel numb, but seeing her lifeless body has strengthened my pledge to her. The Germans must pay.

My packing is done, although I don't remember doing it. I'm going to head east. I'm going to find the resistance fighters and join them. I take the knife from my Mama's hand and kiss her on the forehead. The tears start, and continue as I stumble in the darkness, outside and heading east with a determination I didn't know I possessed.

***

It has been several weeks now. I've traveled at night, keeping to the edges of the road and quickly hiding whenever a vehicle or marching troops approach. This has been rare, as it appears most of the fighting is happening to the north of me. In the distance I see the sky lit with artillery from both sides, arching overhead and exploding like fireworks.

As dawn breaks each day I look for shelter -- some place to hide and to possibly find food. Sometimes I come across hastily abandoned farms where I can dig for potatoes, onions and carrots. I've been fortunate: food has been somewhat easier to find in the countryside than it was in Minsk.

And now, this morning, something different… I smell a cooking fire. I've not lit one since I started my journey, and I realize that I'm not alone. I crawl slowly across the barn floor, avoiding the portion of the roof that has collapsed on the west side. Through a gap in the barn boards I see them outside.

Two men and a woman, all with rifles slung over their shoulders. Their faces and clothing are grimy and caked with dirt. They are gathered around the fire, roasting a rabbit or a chicken. I can hear them speaking in Russian.

"Do you think we succeeded, Igor?"

"We will know soon enough. The train should pass through any minute now and we will hear the explosion."

The woman speaks: "The explosives are on the bridge, just as instructed, and the timer set, just as instructed. We have done our part. If the bomb doesn't go off, we can try again, but I think we have done all we can to make sure this German supply line is put out of commission." She removes a flask from inside her coat, takes a drink, and hands it to one of her comrades.

"You are right, Olga. It is out of our hands. Cheers."

I shift my position to get a better view of the surroundings, and in doing so, a floorboard creaks.

"Vlad… did you hear that? From inside the barn."

One man drops to a crouch. The woman, Olga, and the other man quickly do the same. The three quickly separate and form a semi-circle around the barn door.

"Come out with your hands raised, or we will light the barn on fire."

***

Olga hands me a cup of hot coffee. "Wake up, Sofia. Today is an important day. Today you meet our NKVD contact."

I accept the coffee and smile at my new friend. "I still don't see why you and Igor and Vlad are so anxious to be rid of me. Haven't I been useful? Haven't I fit right in with you three? I think Vlad likes me, too."

"It's not about that," Olga admonishes. "We always work in cells of three. No more, no less. You will be welcomed in your new cell… just as you were welcomed here. As for Vlad, that guy loves any woman who smiles at him."

We share a laugh. At that moment, we hear the signal. The NKDV contact is on the way.

Igor and Vlad enter our camp first, followed by a man who looks oddly out of place. Unlike us, the man is not caked in dust. Nor does he have a rifle. His clothes are too refined for a war zone: a tailored suit, polished black leather shoes, a grey overcoat and matching fedora.

Vlad makes the introductions. "Sofia, this is our NKVD man. We know him as Fedorov."

Federov eyes me with a lidded stare, then speaks slowly in almost inaudible Russian. "The pleasure is mine. I've heard your story. My condolences. You know, I met your father. A very brave patriot."

I'm temporarily speechless. This man met my father. "You met Papa! Oh my goodness. Please tell me it's all a mistake. Please tell me he's still alive."

He does not speak, only shakes his head. I nod, regaining my composure.

Fedorov continues, "If it is any consolation, he died a hero. Now... to business. You understand we will need you in another capacity, correct?"

"I understand you have a rule. I understand I can't stay with Olga, Igor and Vlad and I must join another cell."

"You are partially right. You can't stay with your new friends. But, we have something else in mind for you. Please come with me. I will fill you in on the way back."

"Back? Back where?" I'm somewhat thrown by this new revelation.

"Rule number one: do not ask questions unless invited to." Federov answers curtly, and with that, starts to retreat back through the forest, motioning for me to follow.

I look at my friends. They nod. Olga walks over and hugs me. "Good luck, Sofia. And believe me, we wouldn't put you in the hands of someone we didn't trust. Go, follow Federov. He will help you get your revenge."

And so it is. I am now in the hands of the NKVD, the Soviet Secret Police.

CHAPTER 1
HOMING PIGEON

I'm sitting in the pub enjoying a pint, listening to music playing from a radio perched precariously on a shelf behind the bar. British servicemen and women are dancing, chatting, laughing. It's hard to believe there's a war going on; even harder to believe that less than seventy-two hours ago I was being spirited out of a frozen Norwegian fjord by Navy commandos. Lost temporarily in my thoughts, I am jolted back to reality by a pair of eyes across the room, flashing briefly at me from under a rain soaked hat; his coat collar turned up concealing most of his face. A spook if I've ever seen one. I nod, he nods back, and our silent greeting complete he moves nonchalantly towards the door.

Without a word, I pay the barman, who grunts his thanks for the meagre tip. I get up and follow the spook into the damp and dreary London night.

"How long had you been watching me?"

He answers smartly, "You mean in the bar, or before that?"

"It doesn't matter. What do you want?"

"I have a message for you."

He reaches for my hand; my immediate reaction is to break his nose, but in a smooth motion that he must have practiced numerous times, he slips a small folded piece of paper into my palm. Before I can ask any questions, he smirks, blows me a kiss (clearly his training included being a smart ass) and he blithely vanishes into an alleyway. I hear a guffaw at my expense, and his muffled footsteps fading away as he disappears into the fog.

Back in my room, I unfold the paper. It has two words in typewritten text: "Homing pigeon." This is Intrepid instructing me to return to Camp X.

I sit on the corner of my single bed, staring at the peeling flowered wallpaper in my dismal little room. I am a jumble of emotions. Since I've been in London decompressing from my time behind enemy lines, I've ping ponged back and forth between immense relief that my assignment was over, and then incredible, almost overwhelming feelings of fear and foreboding. Some nights I wake up in a cold sweat, reliving some of the darkest nights of hiding in Norway.

However, these competing emotions are overridden on receiving my instruction. The note of recall has me perplexed and more than a little disappointed. Hadn't I just succeeded in my mission behind enemy lines, where two previous missions had failed? Wasn't I more valuable behind enemy lines causing havoc? Why was I being summoned? With some effort (and a quick snort of Scotch whiskey) I take a deep breath and push these thoughts down. You learn not to question your handler, and Intrepid was even more stringent than most when it came to tipping his hand. You were told only what you needed to know and only when you needed to know it. The less intelligent intelligence officers would take offence, thinking it office politics and a power play by a wannabe alpha male. But, given that Intrepid is in fact THE alpha male (and I'm intelligent enough to know that), I never question his methods. In fact, I'm certain that Intrepid was acting more as a benevolent father figure, keeping me in the dark to preserve me from those same politics and worse.

The next morning I hitch a ride on a merchant marine convoy returning to Canada. HMRS Pickwick averages around eight knots an hour, so I settle in for two and a half weeks of monotony. I'm not disappointed in that regard. The north Atlantic is a grey mass, heaving and swirling, pitching and rolling as far as the eye can see. I spend as little time as possible above deck, the temperature and mist rising from the bow chilling me to the bone within seconds. Sitting in my hammock, bored to tears, my mind is swirling with questions and speculation. At night, I'm greeted with the return of my night sweats and a recurring dream.

The dream always starts the same and always takes me back to that horrible night. We had just completed a successful mission.

A local collaborator, who had been particularly friendly with Norway's Nazi overlords, had been taken off the board in a roadside assassination carried out by my cell. Post mission, the standard operation is to go into hiding for a week or two until the dust has settled. The three of us who formed the mission team split up and I hastened to my prearranged hideout; a dugout shelter hidden several feet below the floor of the local tavern. Claustrophobic, ill lit and damp, but nonetheless safe, given that only I and the tavern owner (also a member of the underground) knew of its existence. After about seventy two hours in hiding, I'm awakened from a fitful slumber by a clamor above my head. I can tell by the shrill German shouting that the Nazi SS had arrived and they are in a very foul mood. It is not long before I hear shots fired. Then more shouting, and more shots. I can picture the impromptu firing squad and the grim resignation of its victims. Sometime later, I smell smoke.

This is where my recurring dream diverges from reality. In reality, before I'm overcome with smoke, I fight against my panic and make my way up the ladder to the escape hatch of my hideaway and, after several tries, and with all the force I could muster, I manage to lift the weight of the floor/door, plus the rug and potted plant that were positioned on top of it. I crawl out and barely escape out the back entrance of the tavern as flames engulf it. In my dream, I'm not so fortunate. In my dream, the smoke seeps into my hideaway, and continues to build as I try, to no avail, to push the door up and open. I scramble back down to the bottom of my hiding place, fighting for oxygen, covering myself with blankets soaked in the water I have, including that from the latrine bucket. I see the flames licking at the door and hear the roar of the flames above me. Pieces of the trap door alight. The heat is incredible. My wet blanket smolders. It is all futile. My skin starts to blister as my lungs gasp and my panic builds and I begin to scream. The flames spread and I'm enveloped in an inferno. This is when I awaken, usually grabbing my throat and huffing like a steam engine, sweat dripping from my body in buckets. I was hoping that the dream would disappear with the thoughts of returning to Camp X and perhaps a new assignment. Maybe the sense of isolation on the ship has just revived my subconscious and the nightmare that it conjures. I shudder to think that I will have to live with this dream.

The ship's crew studiously ignores me. They must have known by instinct that I belong to another world, coming out of the shadows by necessity, not by choice. When we finally reach Halifax, I can't wait to board a train and make my way back to Ontario. The trip takes a total of eighteen days, but seems like eighteen years. In Whitby I'm greeted at the rail station by another spook, who takes careful pains not to advertise it, but, like dogs of a similar breed, we cannot help but sniff each other out. I follow him to his waiting sedan, with not a word between us. We finally reach Camp X and I'm shown into Intrepid's office by a matronly woman as grey as the painted wall, her lips sealed shut in a thin line, and as impenetrable as a vault.

Intrepid looks up from the clutter on his desk. His eyes look tired, but when he speaks, the spark of intelligence cannot be mistaken. He smiles and I am glad to see that he seems happy and relieved to see me. This is a pleasant surprise, and doubly so. Nobody has been happy to see me since my rendezvous with the commandos in Norway, and, for Intrepid to be happy to see me means that my summons was not due to some foul up on my part.

"You look like hell. What took you so long?" he asks in his casual way, as if we'd agreed to an after work drink.

"Hadn't you heard? There's a war on and we had to avoid getting sunk by U-boats." I match his bombast with a bit of my own.

"Well, glad you made it. Have a seat; I'd like to hear your story first, then I'll tell you about your next assignment."

We move to the sofa and he offers me a drink. Sipping on some single malt scotch, I relate in detail my rendezvous with the Norwegian underground (although I leave out my nighttime rendezvous with the Nordic goddess Astrid, who helped keep me warm at night). I describe the various safe houses they had established, including the now burnt out tavern. I then tell him how I managed to infiltrate the hydro plant, touring as a visiting dignitary with one of the local politicians who had claimed to be a Nazi sympathizer (or a 'Quisling' as the locals referred to him), but was in fact a double agent, employed by the resistance. This man had ice running through his veins. His name (or so he claimed) was Orst. Through careful cultivation of Adolf's appointed goons, he'd managed to gain their trust. Once included in their circle, he further ingratiated himself by exposing (read 'framing') another Quisling as a double agent. With Orst as my ticket in, I was able to pinpoint the structural weakness of the hydro generating plant, and then relay what explosives I needed to put it out of commission. Here, Intrepid interrupts me.

"Yes, I recall seeing those requisitions and was surprised you didn't need more to do the job. Did it occur to you what would happen if you only damaged, but didn't totally destroy the plant? That's a rhetorical question; let's just say we would not be having a pleasant chat at the moment."

I take this as a backhanded compliment and continue my story, ending with my delivery to English soil. But at this point, I can't resist making one final observation that I knew would get his attention (but also risk raising his ire).

"I can't help but wonder why this particular hydro plant was such a priority. I heard from some of the looser tongues in the underground that I was not the first spook to turn up amongst them with orders to destroy it. And, I have to say, if the locals spotted them as spooks then it is no wonder they failed. But, that aside, I thought back to the halcyon carefree days of my time at Queen's, studying hard to master various methods of producing energy. And the dots connected like a deciphered telegraph. Heavy water. Heavy water plays an important role in transforming common uranium into weapons-grade uranium – and that's what this is about. The Nazis are trying to build an atomic bomb, right? One that would turn the war in their favour, if my engineering professor's lecture on the potential energy that could be released wasn't pure fiction."

As usual, Intrepid doesn't react in the way I expect. He is not at all surprised. "Of course I knew you would understand what was going on there once you saw the place. I'm sure you didn't sleep your way through all those university lectures. That is one of the reasons I've summoned you back here. Since I speculated that you already know what the Nazis are up to, super sleuth that you are, it would not be a leap of inspired intellect to surmise that our side is working on the same thing."

I shake my head, feigning a bit of surprise at this revelation, but realizing (and yes, surmising as Intrepid had surmised I would) the logic of it all. Of course we are working on an atomic bomb. Intrepid knew that I would eventually arrive at that conclusion. And, of course this would be information of the utmost secrecy. He had summoned me home knowing that I had to be debriefed and brought into the elite circle that knew of this undertaking 'officially' lest my 'unofficial' ponderings cause trouble. Intrepid sent me to Norway knowing full well that he'd be bringing me back. The question now was, what would he do with me? There must be a reason he's shared this information with me officially. Or, was he just preparing me for a period of prolonged exile, not unlike my sullen sea voyage on the very forgettable HMRS Pickwick? In this business, too much knowledge can be a dangerous thing.

"Don't worry. I have no intention of throwing you into the wilderness. We have work to do. Right here, in Canada. I'm going to introduce you to the Twenty Committee. You'll learn all you need to know from them about your next assignment."

With that, he rises from the sofa, and extends his hand. "Someone will collect you soon. Until then, go home. Be with your grandparents and enjoy some time to decompress. You've earned it."

I leave his office feeling a mixture of pride and trepidation. Pride in a mission accomplished and acknowledged, and the faith that Intrepid has shown in me by sharing classified secrets; but also trepidation in my imminent return to the grey world of espionage and what that future might hold. I'm not familiar with the 'Twenty Committee' and I'm very curious about its purpose and what my involvement will be. And something else nudges at me, just below the surface. I can't quite put my finger on it, but it is an anxiousness. The thought of returning home should delight me, and in many ways it does. But I can't help feeling that somehow it will be strange for me and for those who know me. I know I'm not the same man I was when I left home three years ago.

CHAPTER 2
FINEGAN

The cover story that my grandparents were told was that my hearing had been impaired during a training exercise involving heavy artillery. Not a flattering story, but, believable nonetheless. This had earned me a medical discharge and a ticket home. The conquering hero indeed. It is a cold March day, overcast and damp, when I am dropped off at the end of our farm's quarter mile long driveway.

Despite my lackluster cover story, both of my grandparents cannot suppress their joy at my arrival. And, in spite of their advanced ages, both practically sprint to meet me halfway, laughing and throwing their arms around me, as the family dog, Tipper, dances around all of us, barking with all the excitement. It is a joyous reunion, but one I had hoped would have signaled the end of the war, not the beginning of a new clandestine assignment. The anxiety I had felt in Intrepid's office is temporarily at bay.

It's been a few weeks and I'm restless but trying to settle back in to my old surroundings. And now, as we sit by the fire in our modest yet warm and inviting parlour, my grandfather nods in my direction, and speaks in a tone of quiet confidence, "Marcus, your Norwegian has vastly improved. In fact, it sounds more natural than mine and reminds me of the old country. Tell me, how would this happen with your assignments in England?" The sly fox. Perhaps genetics played a role in my recruitment for the secret service.

Of course, being as sly as my grandfather and then some, I was prepared for this question. I had a convincing fabrication at hand. "Well, Bestefar, my unit was composed mostly of expat Norwegians. As you know, many able-bodied men fled Norway during the Nazi invasion, and made their way to England. The British have recruited men who are filled with vengeance in their hearts, from all of the Nazi held countries."

"But, why aren't you part of the Hastings and Prince Edward Regiment, like all the other young infantry men from around here?"

"Because I'm bilingual. The Officers in our regiment, all Sandhurst graduates and dandies of the British aristocracy, speak only English. They needed lowly men like me as an interpreter so the Norwegian men could follow orders, and I in turn could parlay their grumblings back to the overlords. That's part of the reason I made Lieutenant so quickly. I'm just disappointed I won't be with my men when we give Adolf a black eye and liberate Norway."

I glance at him and see a faraway gleam in his eyes. I think he is also sad that he could not be there, leading the charge, despite his years. He nods slowly, then speaks in his soothing voice, "Do not be disappointed. You have done your part and, I don't need to tell you, you are needed here on the farm. We have lots of work on the home front to do if we want our lads fed and looked after. They are counting on us."

I think how right he is, even more so than he realizes. It is not just the men in arms that need our help. The civilians caught up in the war have also suffered greatly. I can hardly look at a child now after witnessing some of the malnourished, pitiful refugees I have seen in England and occupied Norway. This war is being fought on many fronts; some much closer to home than my grandfather knows.

I get up and throw another log on the fire. The hiss and crackle from the cedar, augmented by the brandy grandfather handed me after dinner, adds to the mellow atmosphere. I glance at my grandfather and notice the telltale head bobs of a man ready for bed. "I'm feeling a bit restless, Bestefar. I think I'll take the truck into town and have a couple of beers with the lads."

"You do that, Marcus. I'm heading off to bed. Throw another log on the fire when you come in, ok?"

"Will do. Goodnight."

"Goodnight."

I bundle up in my army-issued leather bomber jacket, grab the keys to our old Ford and head out. It is around nine-thirty p.m. on a Saturday night – a time I had relished before joining the service. The drive from our farm into Port Hope is a short one, barely enough time for the Ford's engine and passenger compartment to warm up. I pull into a parking space across the street from the Ganaraska Hotel, turn up my collar against the wind blowing in from Lake Ontario and head towards the entrance.

The familiar smells of cigarettes, beer, and fried food mingle with sweat and perfume. A few men wearing uniforms and five o'clock shadows pause their pool game and nod their heads as a way of recognizing a fellow vet; one even gives a lazy salute, respecting the Lieutenant stripes on my shoulders. I return a lazy salute, a message of 'at ease' silently imparted. I make my way across the room, smiling and nodding to familiar faces of friends and acquaintances, some surprised to see me, many already having heard the town gossip of my return and the circumstances that made it necessary. Conquering hero indeed. I pick an open spot and sit at the bar, catching Lainey's attention. She is a friend from high school who now makes her living slinging beer at the Ganny and driving the bar flies to distraction.

"Glad to have you back, Marcus. What can I

get you tonight?"

"Whatever is on tap, Lainey."

She grabs a pint glass and begins to pull a beer for me, watching me out of the corner of her eye. She plunks the beer down in front of me, not even pretending that a coaster is necessary, mumbling, "On the house, Lieutenant". She moves on to her next customer, who quickly redirects his eyes to her cleavage. Now twenty-six and never married (nor desirous of that state), I felt Lainey always seemed to be sizing me up as a potential notch on her bed post. Admittedly, I'd been tempted more than once, but now duty comes first and I am in no hurry to have a relationship, despite her very obvious appeal. I get the impression she is still a bit steamed at me for rejecting her last attempt at seduction (over four years ago), but that is all for the better because I'm not here for entertainment or romance, and certainly not with someone who holds a grudge.

I had been instructed by Intrepid to look daily in the Port Hope Evening Guide want ads. That was all he said on the matter. I had been checking religiously every day, scanning through volumes of 'for sale', 'room for rent', 'help wanted' and the occasional lonely heart's lament, when last Thursday I spotted an ad that simply said, "Glider Molson 9pm Monday". Glider was my cover name. Molson was the Ganny. Monday at 9pm actually meant Saturday at 10pm. My contact was reaching out. And now, here I was at the appointed time in the appointed place.

I sit nursing my beer, making small talk with some of the usual bar flies, and doing a verbal dance with Lainey who seems to be slowly thawing. A corporal approaches and slides down onto the seat beside me. After a sip of his beer and a cursory glance at Lainey (mandatory as cover I assume), he talks quickly under his breath. "The weather in Brussels is gloomy." I answer in a similar vein, "But Paris is very sunny." We've exchanged our secret greeting, one I used with Intrepid on several occasions. The ball is now in his corner. Speaking in low tones to stymy any potential eavesdroppers, he utters, "I'm going to get up and leave. Wait one minute, then follow me out. I'll be in a black Chrysler sedan. I'll flash my headlights when I see you exit the bar. Follow me in your truck."

He gets up and exits, and I leave as instructed. I see headlights flash to my left as I make my way to my old Ford. He heads south and turns right onto Walton Street. We continue on for several more minutes until we hit the outskirts of Port Hope. It's pitch black, with a waning moon, its pale reflection off of the snow banks offering the only light during wartime black out. He finally turns right into the laneway of a farm that has long ago been abandoned; used now primarily as a make out spot for the local high school kids in the summer and completely ignored in the winter. Ignored, apparently, by all except this man and the field mice looking for some warmth. He gets out of his car and, without a word, points like the ghost of Christmas future to a structure on my right, then he pivots, returns to his car and silently drives away, his dimmed lights disappearing back into town.

I start towards a barely discernable outline of a barn, gingerly taking my time in the darkness. The smell of barn board and the darkness suddenly transport me back to my hideaway in Norway. I freeze as a tremor takes hold. I make fists so tight that I feel my finger nails biting into the palms of my hands; my eyes shut so tight I see stars. Gradually my breathing calms, I open my eyes and return slowly on my path towards the barn. As I get closer, I can see a small shaft of light peeking out from under the barn entry door. Cautiously I open the door a crack and peer in, my faculties on high alert. The light is actually coming from what appears to be an old granary in the far corner of the barn. I continue my approach when a voice startles me, "We've been expecting you. Please come along and do make it quick. I'd like to get out of this chill before this fire dies and we all freeze."

Robotically, I do as I am told and hustle over to the granary, stepping inside without hesitation. The glow from the kerosene lamp lights the space adequately enough to make out Intrepid there with another gentleman, presumably the one who spoke. Both are huddled close to a wood burning stove that I can tell is of the portable army variety, hastily put in place. I join them by the fire, and nod to Intrepid.

Ever the gentleman, Intrepid makes quick work of introductions. "Glider, let me introduce you to Finegan. He's to be your contact from the Twenty Committee. Finegan, do you mind bringing Glider up to speed?"

"Not at all, and a pleasure to meet you, Glider."

We shake hands and I am pleasantly surprised by the warmth and the grip of the man. He looks to be roughly forty-five years of age. He wears an overcoat and a bowler hat that makes him look somewhat out of place, and as he speaks I get the distinct impression that he has no intention of staying in small-town Port Hope. In fact, it seems likely he'll be out of the country before the morning sun rises. He has stubble forming on his roundish face that reveals a man who has little time for hygiene. His eyes, on the other hand, are sharp and attentive, darting around the room incessantly, taking in every detail. He reminds me of Intrepid and I know at once he is a senior officer in His Majesty's Secret Service.

He begins his story with a short recap of my Norwegian adventure and a hint as to my future endeavours: "So, bloody good show in Norway. That should cause Hitler and his band of psychopaths a headache. But we aren't out of the woods yet."

By this, I assume he means the Nazis have not given up on their pursuit of an atomic bomb.

"I can't help but notice that you used the term 'we'. Does this mean that I am to be part of another operation, presumably to get 'us' out of the woods?"

With a studied reluctance to answer my question, he asks me a question, "Tell me, Glider, are you familiar with the Eldorado plant in Port Hope?"

It's not the question I expect coming from someone who clearly is not resident in Port Hope. But, like an anxious school boy, I answer as best as I can. "I know of it. Actually, some of the guys I went to high school with work there now. I know it's some kind of refinery, but honestly, I couldn't tell you much about what they do."

Finegan obligingly plays headmaster to my school boy. "Well, let me fill you in then. The short answer is, they refine radium into uranium."

I play dumb, despite an inkling of where this is going. Finegan switches roles from headmaster to history lecturer.

"Initially, uranium was sold into the ceramics industry to manufacture pottery with long-lasting colours. Sounds very innocent, doesn't it? But, in addition, there were sales and loans of uranium products to research laboratories that were exploring nuclear energy for possible use in weapons and power generation. I understand your Queen's engineering classes touched on some of the theories and experiments that Enrico Fermi from Columbia University had published?"

"Yes, I recall some of those lectures." Actually, I recall bits and pieces that managed to lodge in my subconscious brain between naps; but no point in clarifying. Finegan's story is in full gear.

"Good, then. So flash forward to now… 1944. That plant has become one of the most important installations in our war effort, and what they do there and how they do it are secrets that we cannot afford to let slip into the wrong hands. In fact, no single person at the plant understands the entire process. It's compartmentalized to such a degree that it would take months for someone to fully understand it all and document it."

"I'm with you so far." Sort of.

"Well, roughly six weeks ago we intercepted and decrypted a message meant for Erich Schumann. Are you familiar with that name?"

"Sounds familiar, but I can't place it." I hide my surprise at their ability to intercept and decipher encrypted messages. Intrepid catches my eye and I can see he's amused at my attempts to shield my surprise. Again, if he didn't want me to know, I wouldn't.

"Schumann is a leading physicist in Germany… and he happens to be a pal of Reichsmarschall Hermann Goring."

"So, let me guess. The Wehrmacht under Goring is sponsoring work by Schumann and others to build an atomic bomb." I've leapt to the ranks of star student, and Finegan is smiling warmly at his new protégé.

"Correct. Anyway, this message caused a bit of a

kafuffle at head office. You see, we have reason to believe that someone is passing along information about Eldorado's processes onto Schumann via the Swedish embassy. Furthermore, we know that although Sweden is neutral, the current ambassador to Canada, Svend Salming, is a Nazi sympathizer. We are almost certain that he is the person transmitting from the embassy given his sympathies, and how simple it would be for him to do this."

At this point, I have heard enough to understand the gravity of the situation. Yet I couldn't fathom why they were talking to me about it. Why not arrange for the Swedish ambassador to have an unfortunate accident? After all, the roads in Canada can be quite hazardous in winter. However, like Intrepid, I know this man would not think that way. Clearly, he has another plan in mind. One more nuanced and, in all likelihood, more beneficial to our war efforts. I keep my mouth shut and let him continue. I'm greeted with another leading question.

"Glider, are you familiar with the Twenty Committee's work?"

"No, I haven't the foggiest. Remember, I've been in Norway for almost two years, and I don't recall learning of this committee when I was trained at Camp X."

"Right, well, the Twenty Committee is also often referred to as Department XX, the Roman numeral for twenty. In short, we look for opportunities to double cross or 'XX' enemy assets and use them to further our cause." Finegan looks very pleased with the cultural gymnastics it takes to connect Twenty Committee to ancient Rome. I'm far more blunt.

"I see. So, you are counter intelligence specialists."

"You catch on quick." He seems a bit nonplussed that I didn't share in his clever double entendre.

"Thank you." I smile and am greeted with a return smile. A twinkle in his eyes tells me that he quite relishes his work, and that my blunt remarks are forgiven. Now, I sense, is where the rubber will be hitting the road. I'm not disappointed.

"Here is our plan and where you come in. We'd like you to first off find out who at Eldorado is passing information to our Swedish friends. Once we know that, we believe we will be able to persuade that individual to work on our behalf. And once that is accomplished… well… let's just say the Wehrmacht and its physicists could be in for a nasty surprise." His face is transformed. He's like a chef who's just lifted the silver top off his gourmet meal and expects a round of applause. I act like a patron who expected surf and turf and is being served baked beans.

"You make it sound simple. You do realize that Eldorado employs hundreds of people. Further, as you yourself noted, the process is compartmentalized. How do we know where to start? It sounds very much like looking for a needle in a hay stack."

I can tell that what I said is not very much

welcomed. However, I can also tell that my new friend from Department XX isn't finished yet. He holds up his hands in a gesture akin to his school master persona, quieting a class room, and then continues.

"Well, you already sound a bit defeated, but be patient; you haven't heard the rest. We've done some ground work for you. You will be happy to know that we've had a chat with the Plant Manager and with the head of the Personnel department. You've been hired on as an engineer and will begin work next Monday. Congratulations."

He smirks at this, clearly finding my reaction amusing. I sit dumbfounded as he carries on. "Further, we have narrowed down a suspect list for you, which I've arranged to drop box for you, along with some technical reading you might want to review prior to Monday. Here, take this." He hands me a key. "This is for a safety deposit box at the Port Hope train station. The number is on the key. Henceforth, anything that we want to share with you will be dropped in that box, and vice versa. Anything you care to share with us follows the same route. You will need to check it daily. Lucky for you, the train station just happens to be right up the road from Eldorado, and its parking lot is often used by Eldorado employees. Now, do you have any questions?"

"Just one. How urgent is this?" In this business, like most, timing is everything. Finegan hesitates, over-dramatically in my opinion, but as I listen I realize it is the gravity of the situation more than his flair for drama that causes the hesitation.

"Let me put it to you this way. Your mission in Norway helped buy us some time, but not much. The Wehrmacht is getting close. And, to make matters worse, they are also getting very close to developing another new weapon. An unmanned projectile, capable of delivering explosives from across the channel at speeds we can't even imagine. A deadly combination, wouldn't you agree?"

I now understand the urgency. "Very deadly. No time to waste."

Finegan claps his hands together, to punctuate his lecture. "Correct. You may want to stop at the train station on your way home. Oh, and one more thing. To smooth your way somewhat, the gentleman at Eldorado who has hired you has been made aware of your real purpose and will ensure you get the access to the individuals in the plant that you need. He seems reliable, but you may need to remind him of the delicacy of your mission and the consequences of blowing your cover. His name is Trevor Jinx and he is the Vice President in charge of Personnel."

I hope that my Eldorado contact's name is not going to bring bad luck to our mission.

CHAPTER 3
ELDORADO

I spend Sunday pouring over the information I had retrieved from my drop box. There are two main topics. The first is a series of technical documents, outlining the theories behind atomic energy and some speculation on how best to refine uranium. Dry as cornflakes, but necessary reading. Some of this is a walk down memory lane, since, as Finegan had noted, my Queen's engineering classes had touched on atomic energy theory. However, much of it is very new information to me. From what I can glean, the process requires advanced chemistry, advanced thermal dynamics, advanced physics, and advanced math to truly comprehend. Intellectually, I am in way over my head, being not advanced in any of those topics (or any others come to think of it). However, I do manage to cobble together a remedial understanding of the overall process, which is likely more than most who work in the plant.

The second source of information contains a brief biography of each of the suspects. There are four in total, each holding a senior position at Eldorado Refining Limited, and, in theory, having the security clearance to gather the type of information that had been passed to the Swedish ambassador.

I read each of these bios in turn, focusing on the scant information provided about their lives. Apart from all working at the plant and residing in Port Hope, I learn that the four men have quite different appearances and personalities.

Paul Greer is the President and CEO. He is forty-two and a graduate of the University of Toronto MBA program. He's married to Eleanor and they have two daughters: Diane, aged twelve, and Suzy, aged ten. They live on Dorset Street and attend Saint Mark's Anglican Church every Sunday. Eleanor keeps busy maintaining the household and serving as chairwoman for the local chapter of the 'Women's Institute of Ontario'; a philanthropic organization that raises money, food and other items essential to the war effort. The kids attend the local school and help their mother around the house. In short, the Greers appear to be a typical upper class family in small town Ontario. Of note, Paul is also universally hated by everyone in the plant. He's known to throw his weight around (which is politely described as bulky) and to let everyone within ear shot know who is in charge. He also has a history of hiring unqualified secretaries, meaning not qualified for secretarial work, but he believes well qualified for his roving hands.

Barry Davis is the lead chemist at Eldorado. He is thirty-six years old and was rejected from the military due to arthritic knees. He walks with a cane and, from the photos, looks much older than he is. He is single and lives in an apartment above Happy Home Bakery on Ontario Street, right down from the Ganny. His only interest outside of work appears to be his membership in the Masons. He's described by his co-workers as a taciturn, standoffish, moody intellectual snob. A real peach.

Randal Schock is an electrical engineer and head of plant maintenance. Randal was a widower, and emigrated with his daughter from Hungary in 1938. At fifty-two he is the eldest of the suspects, and lives in a large house on Pine Street with his divorced daughter, Agnes, who is aged thirty-one. Randal belongs to the local Europa Club and frequents the Ganaraska Hotel, where he often drinks until closing time. The Europa Club is composed mostly of Italian, Austrian and Hungarian emigres, many of whom have come to Canada in the last decade. Schock sounds like the exact opposite of Barry Davis: gregarious, outgoing and generous to a fault, he's been known to buy rounds whenever good news from the war front is reported in the Port Hope Evening Guide. Some find this patriotic gesture endearing, others less charitably say that he is showboating, and compensating for the fact that his homeland, Hungary, is friendly with the Fuhrer.

Lastly, Darren Wilson is a mechanical engineer and is in charge of materials handling and workplace safety. He is twenty-eight, the youngest of the suspects. At sixteen, Darren lost his left hand when his clothing was caught in a tractor's rear power train outlet, making him unsuitable for military duty. He too is unmarried, although rumoured to be seeing none other than Randal Schock's daughter, Agnes. Like Randal, Darren spends many evenings at the Ganaraska Hotel and lives just up the hill from there on Brown Street. Some at the plant find irony in the fact that a one-armed man is in charge of handling anything, however, this little joke is not mentioned in his presence. Darren is known to have a temper and never forgets a slight. He's also notoriously cheap.

After going over all the material a second time, I make my way to bed, my eyes heavy and my mind spinning. My grandfather and grandmother had promised that they'd wake me in time for breakfast and drive me into town for my first day of work. They were very pleased when I told them how much I'd be making, and with my promise to hire someone to help around the farm.

Hearing my grandmother's call, I wake Monday morning with the usual trepidation that I experience when starting a new assignment, heightened by the lack of sleep due to another visit by my recurring nightmare. After a solid breakfast, my grandfather passes me the keys to the Ford, "Take it. I won't need to go anywhere… and if I do I can always take the tractor." A break for me, as I can now come and go today as I please.

I arrive before the morning shift's scheduled start. The security officer at the front door had been informed of my start that day and leads me directly to Mr. Jinx's office. After brief introductions, Jinx shuts the office door and directs me to a chair across the desk from his. He is a short, lean man, with beady eyes behind coke bottle glasses, a receding hairline and a wispy grey mustache.

I decide to jump right in to our business at hand. "So, Mr. Jinx, I'm given to understand you are aware of my real purpose for being here."

"Yes, this entire arrangement has been orchestrated by a very shadowy figure who introduced himself as Mr. Finegan. I have to tell you, I'm not at all pleased about it, but I feel I of course have no choice in the matter."

Jinx acts like an anal-retentive librarian who has had their quiet world invaded by a group of rowdy teenagers. He frowns over his glasses at me, his loathing barely concealed. I, in return, have taken an instant disliking to Jinx, and I make sure he knows it.

"Correct, you have zero choice. And, let me remind you, should you decide to tell anyone about this, you could find yourself behind bars or worse. Do you understand me, you little twerp?"

He blanches. He clearly isn't used to taking orders, particularly in his own domain. To drive home who is in charge here, I feel I need to rattle him just a bit more. I guess intimidation is now a part of me... it comes second nature.

"Listen to me, Jinx, and listen well. I'm here to deal with a threat to our war efforts. So, you are either going to assist me and keep your thin-lipped mouth shut about it, or you will be treated like an enemy combatant. That means no hearing, no trial… you simply get marched away and thrown into a camp until the war is over. And, let me tell you, Jinx, those camps are no fun, especially for little turds like you. Now, are we clear?"

That little lecture sure gets his attention. I can see the fear as his beady little eyes widen and his jaw goes slack. He regains his composure and quickly responds, "Perfectly clear. I will do anything it takes to make your stay with us a success, and you have my word that nobody, not even my wife, will ever know what your real purpose is here."

I'm surprised he's married and notice his wedding band for the first time. Maybe I've been too hard on the guy. My adjustment to being at home is a work in progress. I often read threats where none exist or behave aggressively when a more nuanced approach would be more effective. I can't say I'm happy about these changes in my personality. I do hope that the longer I remain home, the more I will shed these traits that were acquired while overseas.

I soften my tone and attempt to console Jinx. "Good. Now, if you'd be so kind, I'd like to meet all of the management team. I assume that is standard procedure when a new engineer joins the company?"

"Yes, Mr. Andersen. I've set aside the entire morning specifically for that purpose."

"All right then. See, that wasn't so hard." I give him my most beatific smile.

His face is sullen, but that is fine by me. He gets the message and will be a help, or at least not a hindrance, in my efforts. Frankly, I think he will hide in his office for the 'duration of my stay' as he so adroitly put it. He gets up from behind his desk and leads the way to his door.

Our first stop is the office of the President and CEO, and the first suspect, Paul Greer. His secretary is busy filing her nails. Jinx eyes her suspiciously. No doubt she was not someone hired via his Personnel department. She ignores us like someone who hasn't a care in the world and we take it as a sign to just go right in to Greer's office.

A slight rap on the door gets Greer's attention and, without looking up from his desk, he signals us in. From my vantage point, I can see he's a hefty man with broad shoulders and a barrel chest. He has black hair peppered with silver streaks. His face is dominated by bushy eyebrows and a nose that indicates a man familiar with drink; ruptured blood vessels giving away his vice. His mouth is a slit, pulled back in a frown as he concentrates on his reading. We wait a few minutes while he finishes reading, then when he looks up Jinx introduces me, like a page introducing a peasant to His Highness.

"I beg your pardon, Mr. Greer. I'd like you to meet our new engineer, Marcus Andersen." Jinx smiles so broadly you'd think he was showing off a prize winning steer at the 4H club.

Greer appraises me, raising one bushy eyebrow, and then frowning. Does he seem suspicious, or that just my paranoid imagination? Is it possible he's already figured out why I'm here? He catches himself and quickly regains his composure.

"Andersen, welcome aboard. Jinx has filled me in. Impressive resume. I suppose the army's loss is our gain, and God knows we need all the help we can get. I understand you are somewhat of an efficiency expert and this new position will help us expedite our processes?"

"Yes, that's right, sir."

"Hmm. Interesting. So, how does an army lieutenant/engineer become an efficiency expert?"

I can tell from the line of questioning that Greer is sceptical and, based on my reading, he's also keen on putting me in my place. Luckily, I assumed he'd likely have this attitude, and I'm prepared for this unofficial job interview. In my most deferential way, I answer his question/challenge.

"First of all, thank you so much for this opportunity, Mr. Greer. I've heard so many wonderful things about this plant and your leadership. As to your question, well, engineering is a catch-all phrase in the army, sir. While my Queen's Engineering degree did come in handy overseas, the work there was far more practical. You see, the biggest challenge facing any army is logistics. How do you feed, clothe, arm and move thousands of men? And how do you keep doing that, day in and day out while the position of those men is constantly changing? I've spent months working on these questions under different scenarios; honing in on bottle necks and figuring out how best to get rid of them, go around them or go through them. If I may be so bold, those skills can be put to good use in any manufacturing environment."

He raises his eyebrows and a hint of a smile emerges. He lifts his not inconsiderable bulk from his desk and holds out his meaty hand. We shake and I thank him for his welcome (all but kissing his ring), assuring him I will do my best to make Eldorado run like a finely tuned machine. I think I've made a good first impression; unfortunately, I can't say the same for my impression of him. Perhaps it's a prejudice, but seeing a man of his girth in a time of war rationing doesn't sit well with me. Is he buying from the black market? If so, where is the money coming from?

After a few more introductions to other high ranking officials who seldom visit the factory floor, we leave the executive area. Here, Jinx pauses.

"We're going to meet Barry Davis next. Be careful with him. If anyone is going to blow your cover, it will be him. Don't mistake the social awkwardness for a lack of intelligence. He's sharp and very observant."

I'm grateful for the warning. Jinx seems pleased with himself. This information coincides with the brief I read. We make our way down a gang plank that puts us at the southwest corner of the factory's ground floor. A number of windowed offices run along the wall, the first being that of Barry Davis, who is at his desk and appears to be in deep thought.

Jinx knocks on the open door. "Excuse me, Mr. Davis, I'd like to introduce you to someone." I note that we'd interrupted him studying some type of graph. He sighs heavily and barely suppresses an eye roll, not bothering to conceal his pique at us disturbing his intellectual endeavor.

Jinx continues, "This is Mr. Marcus Andersen. He's an efficiency expert here to see how we can increase productivity."

"A pleasure, Mr. Andersen." He's dismissive. "I'm not sure where our paths might cross here; after all I'm a chemist, not at all involved in the hands-on processes here. I'm guessing you'll be spending more time with shipping and receiving and our plant manager than with me."

"The pleasure is mine, Mr. Davis. And please, call me Marcus. I suspect you're right, but I may need to ask you some questions specific to the use of those chemicals, and the processes themselves, once I start to dig a little deeper." Telling a self-described genius that they are 'right' is music to their ears. A very simple way to get them on your side, and, as they say, you get more flies with honey than you do with vinegar.

"Hmmm. Perhaps. And you can call me Barry." And, with that, he returns to studying his charts, leaving us to show ourselves out.

Jinx offers, "Don't be offended that he didn't get up from his desk to shake your hand. He's a bit anti-social. That, and his arthritic knees, keep him mostly at his desk."

My first impression of Davis is that of a sharp customer who keeps to himself. Was this low profile something he honed to allow him to avoid suspicion? Hard to say, but his intelligence alone makes him a suspect.

After several introductions to some of the men on the factory floor, we finally catch up with Randal Schock. After Jinx makes the usual intros and gives a brief blurb of why I was hired, I reach for his hand. "How do you do, Mr. Schock?"

"Sorry, Mr. Andersen, no offense, but my hands are covered in grease. I was just working on that conveyer – had to replace some of the bearings. We've got to get this line up and running again."

"No offense taken. But a quick question, if I may. How many of these types of breakdowns do you get in an average workweek? I mean the kind that shut down the line."

He looks at me, surprised by the question. He's a wiry guy, below average height with squinty eyes, a ruddy complexion and a receding hairline. Although he is a fairly recent immigrant from Hungary, I do not notice a strong accent as he answers.

"I'd say maybe one every couple of weeks that stall production, but several minor ones weekly. We're at war, so some parts, like new bearings, are hard to come by. We grease everything every shift, but they don't last indefinitely."

"And what about those massive boilers... ever have any problems with them?"

The plant floor is dominated by several large boilers. These structures look to be about three stories high. From my reading, I assume that they would be used for thermal diffusion; a high pressure high heating that is the key to the refinement process.

"No, thank goodness. If those ever go, we're all in a lot of trouble." He smiles, as if being in a lot of trouble would be a good thing.

It is a subtle hint, but nonetheless a clue that Schock knows more about the uranium refinement process than a maintenance man might generally know. My impression is that Schock is underemployed. He could likely run this plant if he had to. And, given that he and his staff maintain the entire complex, there is no doubt he has access to information from all areas of the plant as well. We take our leave, with Schock smiling widely. I'm surprised he doesn't hug me. He lives up to his reputation as a very sociable man.

We catch up with the last of my suspects in the shipping area. Or, more accurately, as he is leaving the shipping area. Darren Wilson ambles out of the 'restricted' area that is reserved for those with shipping access. After Jinx introduces us, he shakes my hand with a solid grip from his remaining hand. He's a handsome young man. Tall, lean, with dark hair and a ready (but oddly mocking) smile.

"A pleasure, Mr. Andersen."

"The pleasure is mine, Mr. Wilson. Call me Marcus."

"You know, Marcus, we might have been at Port Hope High School together. You were a couple years behind me, I think. You enlisted, right?"

It's funny, Port Hope is a small town, yet I couldn't recall ever meeting Darren in school, or anywhere else for that matter. And yet, he knows me. That makes me somewhat suspicious, but, like I said, it's a small town. I bluster my way through the conversation.

"Yes, I did enlist, although I was discharged before my unit saw any action."

"Were you with the Hasty P's? I've got a few

friends in that unit."

The 'Hasty P's' is the nickname for the Hastings and Prince Edward Regiment that most of the locals are recruited to. "No. I was working with the English army and their Norwegian brigade. I speak the language and they needed an interpreter, so I got that assignment." I had to be careful here. What if Darren was our man and he contacted someone in German intelligence to see if my story checks out? I'm sure Intrepid would have altered the military records in order to back up my cover story, but sometimes documents aren't enough. There could be Quislings in that Norwegian brigade in contact with the Abwehr who could blow my cover. I improvise, "I was a bit of an oddball. Not Norwegian nor English. I kept to myself quite a bit, but that's all in the past now. I did my duty and now I'm happy to be home."

Now it was my turn to ask some questions. "So, tell me, Darren. In your role of Head of Materials Handling... outside of shipping and receiving, is there other handling that you look after?"

He looks at me like I've insulted him or belittled his position, and I can see that his reputation for being quick to anger is well earned. But in a flash he quickly regains his composure and smiles awkwardly.

"Well, I suppose the job title is slightly misleading, but, to answer your question, shipping and receiving is the bulk of the job, but I'm also in charge of workplace safety. Make no mistake, Marcus, with the type of material we're handling here, I must take that responsibility very seriously."

So, it appears that Darren Wilson is very aware of what Eldorado's end product is, and the dangers which the product poses if not handled properly. His responsibility for workplace safety gives him access to all parts of the plant… clearly someone who can potentially get his hands on information provided someone coaches him on what to look for.

After several more introductions, followed by lunch with a somewhat sullen Mr. Jinx, I am handed a few binders of orientation reading and shown to my new office. I spend the afternoon skimming the reading material, reflecting on first impressions and planning my next moves. I decide that after work I will go to the Ganaraska Hotel and see if I can find out more about Schock and/or Wilson, the two bar flies of my four suspects.

CHAPTER 4
THE GANNY

As the workday ends, I linger in my office for a while, then make my way to my post office drop box. There is nothing in my box and I have nothing to leave for my contact. Not exactly an auspicious beginning, but I can't expect to hit a home run every at bat. And, after all, I'm new to the Twenty Committee; I'm sure they don't have unreasonable expectations. I drive from the lot and make my way to the Ganny.

As I enter I note Wilson and Schock perched at the bar, with Lainey tending. I catch her eye, and she smiles brightly; which in turn gets Wilson and Schock's attention. They follow her gaze and nod in my direction. I take this as an invitation to join them. Might as well jump into the deep end.

"So, Marcus, how was your first day? Did you find some ways to make us run more efficiently?"

Wilson smirks. His sarcasm is not lost on me. I don't take it personally.

"Nothing concrete as yet, but I have a few ideas I'll be looking into."

Lainey brings me a beer, knowing my usual. "Hey, Marcus. I hear you started work today at Eldorado. Congratulations. Does this mean you'll be staying in town? Maybe we should get together sometime soon…"

I had to hand it to her. No shyness, no games. Just right to the point. It might be a good idea to fit in. "Sure, Lainey. I'd like that. Maybe Sylvan Glen on the weekend? Pick you up Saturday at two?" Sylvan Glen is a pretty park just north of Port Hope, with the Ganaraska River running through it. It is a popular spot for picnics and innocent flirtations.

"It's a date."

Wilson watches as she walks away. "I think she likes you, Marcus."

I nod, noncommittally. I'm not there to chit chat. I'm there to listen. They take the subtle hint and return to their drinks and conversation.

Schock turns to Wilson, "Just like you, Darren. Watching Lainey like a man just released from prison. When do you plan on making an honest woman out of my daughter, eh? You know she expects a proposal."

There is no malice in the delivery. Nor does Darren Wilson take it as any kind of admonishment. It is as though they are bartering and the item up for bid is Schock's daughter, Agnes. I'm more than a little disgusted, but also intrigued.

Wilson swivels in his seat. "Well, Randal, I think you know the answer to that. I need to save some money, then hopefully when I can afford a proper home, we can marry. But things are tight. Between rent, my car payments, food, beer… I'm not saving much."

Schock drains his beer. "Hmmm. Well, that wad of cash I spotted in your wallet the other day doesn't seem to add up to your story. Maybe you're just waiting for Lainey there to take a shine."

Darren Wilson scoffs. I get the impression this isn't the first time this topic has come up in conversation. "All right… that's it for me. I'm heading out. See you tomorrow, Randal. Marcus."

As Darren heads to the exit, I decide to tail him. The comment about Darren's 'wad of cash' has caught my attention. Perhaps he's on the Abwehr's payroll. And perhaps I'll get lucky and spot a handoff of more cash or, better yet, information. Her Majesty's Secret Service isn't the only one to deploy the drop box method; perhaps he'll lead me to his. I shake my head at my own impatience. It is day one on the job… I'm galloping ahead of myself.

I make like I'm going to the men's room, do a ten count, then head out of the bar. I spot Darren's car heading south, then left on Walton. I stay about a hundred and fifty yards back with my headlights dimmed. We get to the outskirts of town going east on Highway Two and Wilson keeps driving. Fifteen minutes later we approach Port Hope's neighbouring town, Cobourg, and he heads right at William Street. He is heading towards Cobourg's downtown area.

I keep a safe distance back, so that when he turns left on University Avenue and parks a short distance down the street I'm able to pull into a spot and observe the building he is entering without his noticing me hunched over in the Ford. The streetlights are off but with the moonlight I can make out his destination.

I leave the Ford and wander over to take a closer look. He has entered the eastern-most door of a triplex. A dim light glows from behind semi-pulled blinds. I creep up cautiously, testing the steps and porch decking as I go, hoping that there will be no telltale creaks alerting Wilson and whoever he is meeting to my presence.

Peeking through the lower part of the window, I spot Wilson. He is standing in the middle of the room, talking with someone I can't see, while removing his jacket and tie. Then he begins to unbutton his shirt and soon, a tall, attractive brunette wearing nothing but a slip and carrying two tumblers of whiskey enters the picture. I abandon my perch, quietly retreating back to curbside. I don't need to see the rest of the show to know what is happening. Nonetheless, I take mental note of the address before I return to the Ford and head back to Port Hope. I also vow to watch Wilson a bit more closely before ruling him out entirely. I still have no idea where his 'wad of cash', has come from. However, I have learned that in addition to having a temper, he's a two-timing creep. I'm sure Randal Schock's daughter Agnes would not approve of his dalliance.

I get home close to one in the morning, tip toe upstairs to my room and set the alarm for seven. So ends my first day on the job at Eldorado. I've met my main suspects and have made some first impressions, but no real progress. I vow to find a way to speed up the investigative part of this operation. The mental spectre of Nazi atomic bombs make swift action imperative.

My mind is not at ease after a day of asking many questions and potentially tipping my hand to my adversary. Following Wilson after work, keeping to the shadows, holding my breath and praying anxiously that a loose deck board, unexpected light or frightened house pet won't give me away, has brought back all of the tension I felt behind enemy lines. I'm home, but I've brought the war back with me. I toss and turn for an hour or so, and finally fall into a fitful sleep.

CHAPTER 5
SOFIA

After he leaves, I run to the bathroom and vomit violently. I've known this was going to happen. In fact, I encouraged it to happen. It was part of the mission, what I was trained to do. But, no matter how much I rationalize or justify my actions I can't help what I feel. Nausea is the physical symptom, but mentally I simply can't begin to explore what's happened. What I've made happen.

It was so easy. When I first came to Canada under my assumed identity, I was placed with a family anxious to demonstrate their Christian charitability to anyone who would listen. They would take me to church every Sunday and introduce me as their "Polish refugee", like I was some type of prize that they were anxious to show off. His interest in me was immediate. His eyes undressing me, every time I walked into a room. My handler, eager for me to make progress, prodded me. And now, in hindsight, he was almost like a pimp, demanding that his whore target this very specific john.

And now, here I am. Alone with my thoughts in a newly furnished apartment in Newcastle. He brought me here to impress me, to show off his wealth, but also to ensure that I will be forever in his debt. Like a whore, I am bought and paid for. A possession. An ornament to be shown sparingly, away from the few people I had met in Port Hope, to be consumed greedily, here in this gilded cage he's built for me. Again, I'm wracked with sobbing. I can't stop crying. I lie on the cold tiled floor. After some time (I'm unsure how long), I get up, determined to move; the action itself part of a ritual that I've learned since the death of my mother. Never stay still. Never linger in your thoughts. This is how you outrun madness.

The nausea has subsided and the tears dried up. I run the shower at a scalding temperature and scrub myself clean. As the hot water runs down my backside, I can still picture him in my mind's eye, hovering over me with a blackness in his eyes that can only be described as pure greed and pleasure. But, I picture something else. I see myself, not as a victim but as the victor. This ignorant, foolish brute of a man, so sure of himself and so wrapped up in his own veracious desires, hasn't a clue that he's being used.

I wrap the towel around myself, too exhausted mentally to get dressed. I finger the canister of undeveloped film. Was it worth it? I degraded myself, but my handler was clear: the information I am gathering has the potential to bring the Germans to their knees. He told me that they will feel the wrath of hell, and hell is what they put my mother though. This is the bargain I've made. This is the revenge I've wanted, been trained to obtain. And what I've traded my body and, in some instances, my mental stability for.

And yet, there is still a hollowness to all of this. An abstraction that simply doesn't feel like vengeance at all. I wish desperately that I would have been trained and redeployed by the NKVD behind enemy lines. Instead, I'm in the homeland of one of our supposed allies. It seems surreal at times. It seems like a tenuous thread between what I had hoped to do to avenge the death of my parents and what I am now doing.

And, what of vengeance? I've been in this country for months now. I've seen how life can be outside of a war zone, and it reminds me of happier times with Mama and Papa and our friends. What would they think of me now? Would they want vengeance or would they want me to leave the past and find happiness?

These thoughts torment me, and anyway, regardless, it is too late. I've made my bed and now I must lie in it. I only wish it wasn't with that pig of a man.

CHAPTER 6
THE HUNGARIAN CONNECTION

I continue to follow Wilson for several more evenings. His movements seldom alter. Work, followed by several beers at the Ganaraska Hotel, followed by a visit to the woman in Cobourg who I find out is named Vera Knap. Vera's husband has enlisted and is currently overseas with the Hastings and Prince Edward Regiment. Clearly, Wilson is taking advantage of a lonely woman. It rankles me more than I care to admit.

There was one variant from this general pattern that helped explain the cash that Wilson had flashed, but this leads to more questions than answers.

It was a Friday night. The Ganny was busier than ever. Schock was in fine form, and had decided that beer was not going to cut it. He had been drinking rye whiskey instead, and at ten p.m. was clearly in no shape to drive home. Wilson offered him a ride and Schock accepted. I discreetly followed them, and was rewarded by an unusual scene for my troubles.

Wilson escorted Schock to his front door, where they were met by Agnes who tended to her very inebriated father. I expected a night of romance but to confirm I peered into the main floor windows, hoping to see what was going on. As I crept up to a back window, which provided a view of the Schocks' living room, what I saw surprised me.

Randal was not in the room and I assumed that Agnes had put her father to bed. She returned to the living room, where Wilson was waiting. She regarded him not with affection, but with hostility. After a heated exchange, she left the room and then returned with a handful of crumpled bills. She threw them at Wilson. He looked at her, shaking his head, then grabbed her by the wrist. He whispered something in her ear, then roughly pushed her down to the sofa before grabbing the bills and making his exit. I caught myself clenching my fists, not seeing Wilson but instead seeing an SS Officer interrogating one of the village women. This flashback was so real, it took every bit of my resolve to unclench my fists and my jaw, to slow my breathing and come back to reality.

I drove home, concerned about my state of mind but also simmering a new-found hatred of Wilson and wondering what to make of this scene. It was obvious that rumours of Agnes and Wilson being somehow romantically involved were inaccurate, although Schock himself seemed to believe those rumours. They definitely had some kind of relationship, but clearly it was not a romantic one. In fact, replaying the scene in my mind, it seemed to me that Wilson is likely blackmailing Agnes. Is this somehow related to my mission? What does Wilson have on Agnes or her father that would somehow compromise one or both of them? Could it be that Schock is the source of the atomic secret leaks we are looking for, and that somehow Wilson has discovered that, and is blackmailing the family with exposure? But, if that is the case, why is Schock so chummy with Wilson? Again, more questions than answers. However, this little drama makes me decide to change focus. It is time to shift attention from Wilson and look more closely at Schock and his daughter. But I won't forget about Wilson entirely. He's obviously unscrupulous and generally an all-round rat. But, if it is blackmail, Agnes has a secret that she appears desperate to hide. And, I'm hoping I'm just the guy to find out what that secret is.

Saturday I make my move. Schock's weekend movements are no surprise. He spends the early afternoon hours at the Europa Club, then moves on to the Ganaraska Hotel. I join him there and we begin to chat. I will give this to Schock, he is as billed - a very sociable guy. After turning down his offer to buy me beers and instead paying for his, I start to drop hints that I am looking for lodgings away from my grandparents and closer to the plant, knowing that the size of his house on Pine Street is more than adequate for him and his daughter. He is also known to take in lodgers. He bites, and like a good fisherman

I'm prepared to reel him in.

"I have just the thing for you, Marcus. Let's have another beer, then you can come over to my place and check out our spare room. You might find it's just what you are looking for."

I had told my grandparents earlier that day that I would look for a place in town to stay during the week so that they could have the Ford truck. I could tell they were conflicted - disappointed, but also relieved. My comings and goings as a teenager were one thing, but as a war veteran something entirely different. Also, I am almost certain that they have heard my nocturnal cries during my more desperate hours reliving my near death experience in Norway. I know they worry about me being alone, and are uncertain on what - if anything- they can do for me. My grandfather said I could keep using the truck; that the vintage Oldsmobile they only drove on Sundays would do in a pinch. At any rate, I assured them I would be home on the weekends and would help out during harvest and planting times when the truck was most needed.

Randal and I finish our beers and head to his place. I'm introduced to Agnes, who quite attractive; shy but pleasant. I feel somewhat protective towards her and hope that whatever that swine Wilson has on her, it isn't going to incriminate her as a foreign agent. But that possibility is real and I have to accept it and carry out my mission. I find myself slightly amused and even a bit disoriented at this soft spot. In my time overseas, I would not entertain the notion of an emotional attachment to someone suspected of being the enemy. Perhaps spending time at home with my grandparents has softened some of my edges. And, maybe with more time, I can leave my experiences in Norway behind.

After a brief tour of the main floor, Schock leads me up the stairs to the second floor.

"Here is the bathroom, shared by all of us. But we will provide you with a wash basin for your room, so it's not inconvenient for any of us. This is my room, and my daughter's is across the hall. Your bedroom is at the end of the hall."

We enter my room and he points out all the obvious, with one feature I think will be very useful for my nocturnal wanderings. "You have your bed, and your dresser, and the night stand and your wash basin are there in the corner. This is your closet, and… you see… I think you will appreciate that you have your own private entrance."

He opens the door next to the closet and there is a fire escape which leads down to the side driveway. I can tell he is pleased with this surprise, his chest puffs out like a bullfighter – and is expecting an equally satisfied reaction from me.

I play my role, matching his enthusiasm, "Ah, this is perfect, Randal. Now the burning question. How much per month?"

"Per month? Well, usually I rent for fifteen a

week, twenty-five if you want breakfast and dinner. Tell you what, if you want a month we'll make it ninety and that will include breakfasts and dinners. "

"Hmmm. I will usually be spending weekends at my grandparents... how about eighty-three per month, with breakfasts and dinners only on weekdays?"

"Deal."

We shake on it and agree I'll take up residence on Monday. The stage is set for me to find out all about Randal Schock and his lovely but troubled daughter Agnes.

After a week of living with the Schocks we have all developed a comfortable, and dare I say, domesticated, routine. I spend a lot of time with Randal and learn a bit about his past.

"So, Randal. What made you want to immigrate to Canada?" I ask as a follow up question to one his many tirades about the state of things in Europe.

"It was political. I was involved with an organization called the Arrow Cross Party. When we started to become popular during the depression it was our policy to tie our fortunes with that of the Germans and to a lesser degree Italy, who were making great strides in shaking off the shackles of the Versailles agreements. You are familiar with those?"

"Yes, I understand that Germany and Hungary paid a steep price after losing the Great War."

"An unfair price, and a burden compounded by the depression. Things were very bleak, but Germany was pulling herself out of the depression. It was an alluring deception."

"A deception? Why do you use that term?"

"Well, as I said, I was a member of the new Arrow Cross party in Hungary. This was a fascist party. But as we started to understand more and more of what Germany was doing – and how Italy was following suit – we realized that perhaps being tied to the Nazis was not a good thing. Unfortunately, by then it was too late. Another political rival held power, and he was only too happy to do the bidding of the Nazis. It seemed my party wasn't fascist enough, and we were harassed by the new government. Then they started to round up the Jews and the Gypsies. You had to be very careful. My parents were Gypsies, or more properly, Roma. Anyway, there was enough trouble that I felt it would be safer for Agnes if we left. We were lucky to get out… thankfully my dearly departed wife's parents had connections and money."

"So, this party… the Arrow Cross Party… it was fascist? And you belonged to it?" Of course, I knew of this party, but as a 'soft' interrogation practice, it's always better to pretend ignorance. Intrepid often drolly observed that I excelled in that department.

"Yes, and I'm ashamed to admit that now. I think we were all a bit naive and more than a little desperate. It was easy to blame the French, English and others for our problems. Little did we know that the Germans and Italians would just cause bigger problems. But, try telling that to some of the guys in the Europa Club. I've learned to keep my mouth shut. Some of them are as bad as the Nazis."

"So, you keep your mouth shut about your past. I get that. Who else at the plant knows?"

"Just you and Darren Wilson. He's like a son to me, and I think Agnes likes him. Maybe one day…" Schock trails off for a moment, then continues. "But there are people in the Europa Club who could make things uncomfortable for me, knowing my past and their respect for Hitler. I have to also worry about internment or worse because of my former Arrow Cross Party association. In English you use the term 'between a rock and a hard place'… well, that is my situation. I hope you will keep this information to yourself."

Schock looks reflective and I get the impression he truly does regret his past in Hungary and some of the choices he has made along the way. Nonetheless, I don't feel any closer to knowing if he's our leak or not. There doesn't seem to be any love for the Nazis, but, perhaps there is a residual resentment towards the Allies and the harsh penalties imposed by the Treaty of Versailles. And, perhaps

I'm not hearing the whole story. The other point of interest is just how wrong he is about Wilson… confiding in him, and thinking that there is a chance of romance between Wilson and his daughter. It doesn't add up at all considering what I had seen transpire. I will need to talk to Agnes and see if she can corroborate some or all of this story.

My opportunity to talk with Agnes alone comes the next weekend. Randal will be out at the Europa Club, hopefully leaving Agnes alone in the house on Pine Street. I will use the excuse of needing my boots if needed.

I enter the house by the fire escape, look about in my room for a few minutes, and descend the staircase. Agnes is sitting by the fireplace, listening to the radio and knitting. She looks at me in surprise. It appears she did not hear me enter the house by the fire escape – I file that away as a good thing for future comings and goings.

"Oh! Hi, Marcus. I thought you were staying at your grandparents' home this weekend."

"I am. I just needed to retrieve my boots, which I thought were in my room… but they aren't there."

"You left them in the front hall closet. But, since you're here, can I get you a coffee or something?"

Agnes has taken a shine to me, and I could

tell she was often lonely. I could play this to my advantage, but once again, the burgeoning of a conscience that has been nibbling around the edges ever since I returned from Norway makes that seem unpalatable, despite that fact that it's quite possible that she and her father are the enemy. That said, I need to find a way to get her to share with me information about her past, and her current situation with Wilson. I can be charming without resorting to romantic overtures.

"I'd love a coffee. It's chilly out there."

She leaves the room. I spot her purse beside her chair and take the opportunity to quickly look through it. Sure enough, there is a stash of cash. Perhaps Wilson was due another payment. After a few minutes, she returns to the living room with a plate of squares.

"Coffee is percolating and will be ready soon. Do you like date squares? We need to eat these before they go stale."

"Only too happy to help out." I help myself to this unexpected treat.

"So, Agnes, what are you up to today? You seem to be housebound. Just so you know, any time you want to get out and about you just let me know…. I have use of the Ford and some gas rations, and I'd be happy to be your chauffeur."

She blushes slightly. Perhaps I need to tone

down the charm. "Well, I spend a lot of my time knitting. It helps to make ends meet, and really, I find it soothing here by the fire. But thanks for the offer. I might just take you up on that when the weather warms up a bit."

"So, someone is paying you to knit? I thought you just did it for fun."

"I do some to donate, some for money. I also sew a lot during the week – piece work for a factory out of Oshawa. They deliver material Monday mornings and pick up finished work Fridays around noon hour. It works out well. But Father doesn't want me to do this; he says it's below me."

"Why would he say that?"

"Well, we were pretty well off back in Hungary. My mother's family was wealthy, you see, and my father… well, he was very good at making friends in high places."

"Really? I had no idea. I mean, he's doing well at the plant. He's got a very good paying job and a respected position. But I wouldn't say he had friends in high places."

We both share a laugh, then Agnes tells me more. "Before Hitler annexed Austria, Father was part of a political movement in Hungary. They were trying hard to get Hungary back on her feet… Just like every country, the depression caused a lot of suffering and a lot of political upheaval. Anyway, I guess you could say my father backed the wrong horse in a political race. He started to get harassed by the new government and my mother's parents thought it would be best if we left Hungary for a while. Then the war broke out. Now we aren't sure if we'll ever return there."

"So do you still have family back there, in Hungary?"

"Of course you know that my mother died before we came here. My grandparents died in an automobile accident about six month after we left. As for my father's family, most of them disowned him. You don't marry out of the Roma community and expect to be welcomed again."

"So, you have no ties anymore. But, what of your father's political friends? If you wanted to go back, wouldn't they help?

Agnes sighed. "Please, Marcus. No more. I don't want to talk of Father's politics. Suffice to say he made some mistakes. Nobody in Hungary would be happy to see him and nobody in this country would understand his former political ties."

I can see the distress on her face and there is no doubt she is sincere in her desire to stop this little romp down memory lane.

"Okay, Agnes. Sorry, I didn't mean to pry. I just find the whole topic very interesting. Europe is so different from here in so many ways."

"Yes… but in many ways different is not good. Ah, the coffee!" Agnes takes the opportunity to discontinue this conversation and fetch the coffee from the kitchen as I mull over what she's told me. Over black coffee, we chat about mundane things, making small talk, and after a short while I retrieve my boots and take my leave.

She has corroborated much of what her father had said, and I now have an understanding of where her money is coming from. The only unknown was why she is unhappily handing cash over to Wilson. It is still possible that it is blackmail money paid to keep a traitorous secret, but, given the story Randal and then his daughter shared, it doesn't sound likely. I'm no closer to finding out who our Axis spy is. I decide it is time to look closely at my remaining suspect, Paul Greer, the President and CEO of Eldorado Refining Limited, and Barry Davis, the chemist.

CHAPTER 7
THE MASON

I think Barry Davis will be a tougher nut to crack than Schock or Wilson have been. First off, he isn't a social guy. I had followed him for an entire week and the only time he wasn't either at work or in his apartment was when he was attending a Wednesday evening Masonic Lodge meeting or doing his grocery or pharmacy runs. There will be no chance of meeting up with him at the Ganny, or any other establishment for that matter. He seldom leaves his apartment above the bakery. He never meets with anyone, nor does he leave messages in any drop box location. Frankly, I can't think of any social situation where Barry Davis would be approachable. He appears to be the quintessential loner.

That said, observing him at work confirms why he is on the suspect list. Of all of the suspects, given his background in chemistry, he knows the most about the processes to refine uranium and has access to almost all steps of the processes within the plant. In short, there are not many gaps in his knowledge to complete the picture for the Nazi regime.

Perhaps I could enquire about joining the Masonic Lodge, but I don't like the optics. I feel the environment, shrouded in secrecy as it is, will not provide much of an opportunity to insinuate myself into Barry's life. Besides, I don't think men walking around in hooded robes is a good look.

I decide on a different tact with Barry. One that will be more in step with my formal training and less like a gossipy fact-finding mission.

I leave a message in my drop box and am not disappointed when two days later I receive my response.

I had asked for, and received a listening device.
The device is a copy of the Minifon Portable Wire Recorder, which is, ironically, originally manufactured in Germany. The mad scientists at Head Office have taken a Minifon and reverse engineered it. Once they understood this device, it didn't take much for them to modify it for field agent use. The two most important modifications include a microphone that can be screwed in as a working light bulb to any light fixture and, most ingeniously, a thin, almost translucent wire that you can run from that bulb to a sound activated battery-operated recording device. The recording device itself is the size of a pack of

cigarettes and can record up to five hours of conversation. It is a very expensive piece of equipment, but I suppose Intrepid and Finegan think I'm worth it, and I only hope they are right.

I wait until Davis leaves his apartment for his Wednesday night Masonic Lodge meeting. Watching him maneuver himself with his arthritic knees to his car is akin to watching an interrogation I once witnessed where a Quisling had his finger nails removed by one of the resistance leaders. Very slow and painful work. I shudder just imagining his pain.

Once Barry is on his way, I creep up the back fire escape, jimmy the window and enter his private residence.

It is a simple space. A living room, a small kitchen/dining area dominated by a kitchen table and two chairs, a washroom and a bedroom. It appears that Davis has been working at something at his kitchen table. I take a closer look and find several diagrams and mathematical computations that appear to be related to the plant and somewhat suspicious. I remove the miniature camera I have in my coat pocket and snap a few photos for forwarding to Head Office for analysis. Is this information classified? Is he that careless, and am I this lucky? I doubt it, as Davis doesn't appear to be a fool, but, people never cease to surprise, or disappoint, as the case may be. As for me being lucky, well, as my handler has often told me, luck is when skill meets opportunity.

As I continue to survey the apartment, the

perfect hiding places for the microphone and recording device present themselves. In the living room, in the middle of the apartment, is a sofa with a floor lamp resting directly beside it. The sofa has a skirt around its perimeter that reaches to the floor, concealing anything that might be under it – a bonus for dust bunnies and spies.

I have to work efficiently. My goal is to not only replace the bulb, but to also run the wire to the recorder via the lamp's power cord, which runs inside the length of the lamp stand, and extends from the base about six feet. I replace the bulb, then take the lamp apart. I tape the thin microphone wire along the length of the lamp's power cord, then quickly put the lamp back together. I now have the wire running the length of the stand undetected.

I separate the wire for the recording device from the lamp's power cord as it exits the lamp's base. The power cord continues to the power outlet, while I run my translucent wire from the base under the sofa, where I conceal the recording device. I step back to survey my handy work. It is impossible to tell that there is a listening device attached to the lamp, and almost impossible to see the wire and recording device hidden under the sofa. Only if someone moves the sofa or attempts to clean under the sofa and hits the device would they find it. Judging from the dust bunnies huddling under the sofa, that would be a very rare event.

I am satisfied with my night's work as I exit the apartment and descend the fire escape. That said,

I know that if I want to continue to make progress, and of course I do, I can't afford to sit around doing nothing for a week while waiting to retrieve the recording device. I decide it is time to look at the Mr. Paul Greer. Once again, I will need Head Office to assist me, so I make my way back to my post office drop box with some hastily-encoded instructions.

CHAPTER 8
BATTERWOOD

As always, Head Office comes through quickly with my request and I am granted an audience with Vincent Massey at his mansion just north of Port Hope, known as the Batterwood Estate. I arrive early Saturday morning and I'm met at the front door by Massey's butler, who escorts me to the study where Massey is taking his morning tea. As Canada's High Commissioner to the U.K., and as a member of one of Canada's wealthiest families, it is no surprise to see that his home is opulent. The scene is straight out of a Victorian catalogue. Dark paneled walls, ancient hanging tapestries displaying what appears to be a family coat of arms, Persian carpets, vases and other trinkets from Asia, and book-lined shelves on either side of a fireplace. The man himself is seated in a wingback chair facing a hearty fire, morning paper in hand, pipe in mouth.

"Good morning, Glider."

It briefly jars me to hear my cover name uttered by someone I do not consider part of the service, and it must have shown, this instant reaction to fight or flight so ingrained in me. I tamp it down as quickly as I can.

"Uh, Mr. Massey, pleased to meet you. Thank you very much for agreeing to meet with me."

He motions to the wingback opposite him and I sit like an obedient Labrador retriever. Massey quickly puts my mind at ease.

"Not to worry. I've been in the service for many years. My clearance isn't quite as high as yours, but I know enough to help. So, let me see if I have this right. You would like me to organize a gathering of local industrialists and representatives of allied and neutral foreign powers to help promote Canadian exports. I am to use all means necessary to ensure that the Swedish ambassador attends, as well as executives from the Eldorado plant and yourself. Is that correct?"

"Yes, that is exactly correct. I hope you can make this happen. The big question is, how quickly do you think you can you make it happen?"

"Ah yes. I knew that would be the stickler. I understand this is urgent, so I've enlisted my good friend C.D. Howe to help persuade participation." I see a sardonic smile play across his face.

C.D. Howe is Canada's czar of war-time production. He has his fingers on the pulse of all manufactured and agricultural goods in the country. On occasions too numerous to list, he has either promoted or rejected export of Canadian goods abroad, and was highly successful since the war effort takes precedence over everything else. In short, if anyone wants to export goods from Canada, they have to go through C.D. Howe.

"Brilliant. How much did you need to tell C.D. to get him to play along?"

"Minimal. All he knows is that it's part of a secret mission. He understands that coming from me that means something. We are sending out a joint invitation for an event here at Batterwood a week from today."

It is clear that Massey is relishing this. There are many agents in the field who are essentially dormant, until they are not. Massey, given his social connections, is perfect in the role of sleeper agent. And he understands that if Head Office calls and needs access to someone in your social circle, you simple provide that conduit.

We enjoy our tea and discuss matters overseas. As we conclude our conversation, he leaves me with an augmentation to our plan. "One other thing, Andersen, and please don't take this the wrong way. Given that most of the invites are for CEO and board members, your presence will not go unnoticed. A bit above your pay grade, so to speak. So, I have arranged cover for you. You will be escorting my niece to this event. That gives you two reasons to be here; one as an up-and-comer at Eldorado and secondly as a friend of the family."

I appreciate this thoughtfulness. "I do admire a man with a solid plan, Mr. Massey. Thank you very much."

"Not at all. We will see you next week, Andersen. And, maybe when our social gathering is over, you can come by the house and fill me in. I'd enjoy that very much."

"It would be my pleasure. Thank you again."

With that, we part company. I've set up a perfect opportunity, with Mr. Massey's assistance, for the Swedish Ambassador and, perhaps, Eldorado's CEO Paul Greer to tip their hands. This will be a test for me. While working behind lines, I was always surreptitiously looking over my shoulder for enemy agents. The stress was incredible, but, living with it daily became reflex. I was the hunted but now I am the hunter. I decide that prior to the party I will tail our Mr. Greer. Perhaps just the thought of being in the same room with Svend Salming, the Swedish ambassador, will make him panic and reach out for instructions

CHAPTER 9
NADIA

It's a bright and cold Sunday morning. I watch from a side street as Greer leaves his home on Dorset Street. He is alone, his wife having previously left on foot with their two children. Presumably, she is attending church service without her husband.

Greer gets into his Chevrolet and heads out. I follow at a discreet distance, keeping a good distance between my Ford pickup and his Chevy. He makes his way to Highway Two heading west, and after about half an hour he turns onto a residential street in Newcastle.

I circle back and park the car a block away and watch as he disembarks and starts to waddle down the street. Following him on the street at this time of morning in broad daylight is a bit of a risk, but I have no choice. I get out, quietly close the car door, and cross to the opposite side of the street. I keep a distance of about fifty yards between us.

He turns the corner onto a small cul-de-sac, and, just as I'm trying to decide if I should cross over to follow him, I see him climb the front steps to what appears to be first floor apartments of a three-story brick building. I notice 101A beside the left side door and 101B beside the right side door. He knocks on 101A, the door opens and he enters. I decide to wait him out, and find a decent hiding spot away from spying eyes.

An hour and a half later, with my fingers and toes screaming for relief from the cold, Greer emerges. I notice him lean into the doorway to kiss someone. Interesting, but, if he is our man, it seems doubtful that he'd be kissing his contact. Nonetheless, given the wait I've endured, I decide I should see who this mystery person is.

I make my way back to my car, giving Greer time to leave. I have to think of a reason to knock on this woman's door. I decide I need a disguise, so I trace my way back along Highway Two and stop at the local co-op store. I purchase a pair of coveralls, some work gloves, a plunger, a pipe wrench and a drain snake. I don the coveralls over my clothing and make my way back to apartment 101A.

After a few knocks, the door opens and I find myself looking at a beautiful young woman. Her hair is fiery red, as are her lips, her complexion very pale. I'd guess her height at five foot two inches. She wears a simple dress with an oversized sweater, and nylon stockings with no shoes. Even with the sweater, I can see her figure is exceptional. She speaks with what I believe to be a Russian accent.

"Yes. What is it you want?"

"I've come to snake your drains."

"What? What do you mean?"

"The landlord asked me to snake all the drains in the building. It's to clean the pipes. He's worried about winter freeze."

"Okay. Come in."

I enter and quickly take in the surroundings. The apartment is small, but lavishly furnished. The kitchen is well-appointed with new appliances and top end cookery hanging from a ceiling rack. Plates are arranged on an open shelf and also appear to be new.

"Come, I show you the washroom."

I wipe my boots, and following behind her I'm led into the bathroom, which is as impressive as the rest of the apartment. She watches as I run water from the sink faucet.

"This drain doesn't look clogged at all, but I will clear the trap and run the snake down the pipe just in case." I complete this task, and repeat with the bathtub. I plunge the toilet just for show, then we make our way to the kitchen.

I need to make small talk to see if I can gather information about this woman.

"Beautiful place you have here. You must have a wealthy family. Or do you work?"

She stares at me, not maliciously or suspiciously, but with a blank face, like she was thinking of a lie. Finally she answers, "Yes, I work. I am a writer and interpreter."

"Oh, that's interesting. Would I recognize your pen name… Miss…?"

"Mironov. Nadia Mironov. And no, I doubt you know my name. I write and translate Russian poetry."

"Ah. I thought I detected an accent. So, you are from Russia?"

"Minsk. Belarus. Close enough… we are all part of the Soviet Union now."

"Right. Well, Uncle Joe is giving those Nazi bastards hell. It's good we're on the same side."

"Da. Yes."

With that she smiles. And I smile back. She is a very pretty woman. Too pretty. What could she possibly see in the obese Paul Greer? Perhaps his money is the attraction.

I thank her for her time. She asks for a business card, in case she has any future plumbing problems.

"I'm sorry, Miss Mironov, I don't have any with me right now. But if you need me, just call your super. He'll know how to get in touch with me." I make a hasty retreat.

I cruise back to Port Hope thinking of the lovely Nadia Mironov and her possible connection to my mission. I doubt that Russian poetry pays for her lavish apartment and furnishings. It seems likely that Paul Greer is keeping her as a mistress. The thought repulses me, but I can't let that cloud my judgement. I drive by Greer's house and note that his car is back, parked in the driveway.

A thought hits me. I scribble Nadia Mironov's name and address on a piece of paper, asking for any background, and head to my drop box. Back at my room at Schock's I begin to take serious stock of the situation.

So far, I have not made much progress. In fact, I continue to have more questions than answers, and none of the suspects have been cleared so far.

After tailing Greer for almost a week, I've not seen him meeting anyone suspicious other than Nadia, nor has he gone anywhere that might be a drop location. Nadia is a loose end, but hopefully I will know more about her soon. Of course, the party at Vincent Massey's could be his undoing if he's our man.

Schock has admitted that he was at one time a fascist sympathizer. He's also told me that the Europa Club he belongs to is a nest of fascists. So he has the means and the opportunity to gather and pass information, but, as I spend more time with him it doesn't feel right. He legitimately seems uncomfortable – and unsafe – with his past secrets.

Darren Wilson is a womanizer, but again, that doesn't mean he's an Abwehr agent. That said, he appears to be coercing Schock's daughter Agnes. Is it possible that Schock is my man after all, and Wilson somehow knows this and is blackmailing the family? What exactly does he know?

Lastly, there is Barry Davis. Of all the suspects, he is the one I know the least about. His solitary life makes him difficult to get a grip on. Hopefully, the listening device will provide some answers. Soon I'll find out, I hope.

What to do next? I decide to return to Wilson. My plan is simple and could clear a couple of suspects off the list. I will stick to him and the next time he strong-arms Agnes or even her father Randal, I will be ready to confront them. It's a gamble and may blow my cover, so I have to be very careful.

I will also collect the listening device from Barry Davis's residence: Wednesday evening I will make my move.

CHAPTER 10
NARROWING DOWN THE LIST

Darren Wilson spends Monday evening at the Ganny with Randal Schock, then has a late night tryst with Vera in Cobourg. Tuesday night, I get the break I'm looking for. I follow Wilson from the Ganny and this time, he beelines it to the Schock residence.

I quietly make my way up the stairs to my room's private entrance, then creep to the end of the hall and listen to what's going on downstairs. The words are heated, although I can't quite make out what they are saying. It's time to confront Wilson and Agnes.

I descend the stairs quickly and quietly, and catch Wilson roughly clutching Agnes's arm. Wilson shouts, "You will pay me, and now!"

"Wilson, what do you think you are doing?!"

I've surprised both of them, but Wilson quickly regains his composure. "Stay out of this, Andersen. It's none of your business."

Agnes eyes me with a mixture of relief and oddly, fear. "Marcus... it's really nothing. You should leave."

"Not until I find out what's going on. This isn't the first time I've seen Wilson being a brute. Wilson, what's your game? How can Randal say that you are like a son to him, while you spend your spare time bullying his daughter?"

"That's enough, Marcus! You must leave, and you must never tell Father about this. Do you understand?" Agnes is frantic.

"No. No, I don't understand. Maybe you need to tell me more. I'm not leaving until you do."

As I say this, Wilson drops Agnes's arm and comes at me, swinging his prosthetic left arm like a baseball bat. I block his attempted clubbing and land a right uppercut to his chin. He drops to the floor, unconscious before he lands. The adrenaline rush leaves me breathless, and, for a brief moment, I forget where I am, thinking back to a similar confrontation with an enemy operative on another continent. These episodes seem to never let up. Gathering myself, I look across the room at Agnes, who is wide-eyed with horror.

"All right, Agnes. Now, from the beginning.

Tell me why this excuse for a man is demanding money from you. Maybe I can help."

She slows her breathing, her face showing a slow change in attitude from fear to resignation, and motions me to the kitchen. We sit at the table, me with my eyes on the doorway in case Wilson rebounds, and she begins.

"When Father first brought Darren home, I was very pleased. He was handsome and seemed charming and thoughtful, and he treated me very well. Flowers, candy... we dated. He also became such a great companion to Father. Then, one day, it all changed."

"They had spent the day with the Europa Club pheasant hunting. Father was quite drunk, but Randal was sober as a judge. After putting Father to bed, I was sitting with Darren in the living room and he said point blank to me, 'I know your father's secrets... and if you want to keep them secret you will have to pay me, otherwise there are men at the Europa Club who can make your life here very uncomfortable.'"

I interject. "I need to know this secret, Agnes. I need to know what he's threatening you with."

She pauses. "Very well. I will tell you. But you mustn't tell anyone else, or let my father know you know. Promise me."

"I promise." I say this, but I could be lying. I want to help Agnes, but I can't be of any help to her, her father, or to Wilson if they are all part of a conspiracy to help the Nazis build an atomic bomb.

"My father was once very active in politics in Hungary. Do you know much about that?"

I lie again. "Not a lot, no." Sometimes it's better to play dumb. In this way, I can look for contradictions in the story Agnes tells me and the one I've already heard from Schock.

"My father was a leader in the fascist Arrow Cross Party. This was during the depression. He admits now he was mistaken."

"Okay. I understand. But, how does Darren fit into this? Being a lapsed member of a political party in Hungary is hardly material for blackmail."

"He is also of Gypsy, or Roma descent. That is the main reason for our emigration from Hungary. Are you aware that the current government in Hungary is rounding up Jews and Roma and taking them to concentration camps?"

"I've heard rumours of atrocities committed by Nazis, but was unaware of Hungarian complicity. But, again, I ask, why are you so afraid? What is it that Darren has on you two?"

"I'm coming to that. My father's past is like a boat anchor tied to his neck... if he is pushed overboard he dies. There are people in the Europa Club who would look to kill him as a traitor to the Arrow Cross Party and as a Roma. When Darren found out who those people were, he simply threatened to tell them of Father's past. I had no choice but to pay."

"And… who are those people? Tell me. I might be able to help."

"How? How could you help? They are ruthless."

I have to think. Can I trust Agnes? If I tell her about my mission, I could endanger her further. However, if I don't tell her, how can I expect her to trust me? I decide to give her something that resembles the truth, but not the whole truth.

"Agnes, your father isn't the only person with a past. I was not stationed in England while I was away. I was a saboteur, behind enemy lines. I know people who can help you and your father. You have to trust me."

She hesitates. I can see she is connecting the dots, and then arrives at a conclusion. "Very well. The men we fear are Laslo Miclos and Darius Szalsis. Do you know them?"

"No, I do not. Tell me about them."

"Like my father and myself, Laslo comes from Eastern Europe. He is a Serb. The Serbs hold a special hatred for the old Austro-Hungarian Empire and, since the Hungarian participation of the German invasion of their country, with the Arrow Cross Party at the helm, there is no doubt he would take vengeance against my father as a former high ranking official within that party."

I nod. "I see. And what of Darius Szalsis?"

"Szalsis is like us. He is Hungarian. But, unlike Father, he continues to hold to his fascist beliefs. If he knew that my father has rejected his party, and of Father's Roma heritage, he would make life very difficult for both of us. Perhaps he would even kill us. So, you see… we are prisoners of our past. Both men are very influential in their small communities. The conflicts of Europe have followed us to Canada and my father's past makes him a potential enemy of both sides. All we wanted to do was wipe the slate clear and become proud Canadians. But, this bastard, Wilson, holds our secrets over our heads, and knows who to talk to if he decides to harm us. And so I pay him to keep his mouth shut."

I understand now. Her fears are not unfounded. I think of what needs to happen.

"So, Marcus, now you know. What can you do?"

"I will leave now. When Wilson comes to, convince him that you told me nothing. That you claimed it was a lover's quarrel, and that you told me the cash he wanted was for a loan repayment. I promise I will do what I can to neutralize your problem, you have my word."

I leave Agnes and head out for a walk to clear my head. I'm satisfied with her story, and, more importantly, I'm now convinced that Wilson, although a bastard, is not the person leaking information to the Swedish embassy. I'm equally convinced that Schock is not my man. That said, I made a promise to Agnes and now I have to deliver. Randal and Agnes deserve the peace they were looking for when they came to Canada. I come up with a plan, but I will sleep on it and think about when to pull the trigger.

That night, I have another terrible nightmare. I dream this time of an interrogation, only this time I'm not the interrogator or the subject of interrogation. This time, it is Agnes Schock being brutally interrogated and I am a witness, but unable to help her or even present myself as her ally. A tortuous scene unfolds and I'm forced to feign indifference. Finally, I can't take it anymore, and as I make to intercept the interrogator, he turns to me with a gun in his hand and says, "I knew you weren't one of us." He pulls the hammer back, and I abruptly awaken from my dream. I'm panting and sweating, my sheets twisted. After pacing my room for a half hour, I calm down and I'm finally able to go back to bed. After a fitful sleep, I rise in the morning and go to work as usual. I avoid Wilson the entire day, which is just as well – he might say something that could get us both fired. Anyway, Wilson isn't my concern today. Today is Wednesday, and tonight, while Barry

Davis participates in his Masonic Temple meeting, I will retrieve the recording device from his apartment.

After work, I have dinner with Randal and Agnes. Agnes is very quiet. When Schock leaves the table to read today's news in the living room, we make some small talk. She is avoiding the events of the previous evening, and that is fine with me. That said, I feel the need to comfort her. "Don't worry, Agnes. Everything will be fine. I promise." She smiles at me. I think I've relieved some of her tension, and hope that I can live up to my promise. I leave the table and prepare for my night's mission.

It is already dark by the time I'm ready to leave the house. I've got a Swiss army knife, a flashlight, a light bulb and some lock picks. I arrive at Davis's apartment just in time to see him depart in a Port Hope Taxi cab for his meeting. After a few minutes, I retrace my steps from the prior week and make for his back entrance. Within seconds I'm in his living room. I disassemble the lamp, remove the translucent wire, then re-assemble the lamp. I replace the light bulb/microphone with a standard bulb. I grab the Minifon recorder from under the sofa. I'm out the door with my prize and back in my vehicle; the entire process took less than ten minutes. At no point did I feel the paranoia or unease that I've so recently experienced during these nocturnal exploits. Perhaps I'm getting used to being back in the game.

Back in my room, I hit rewind on the Minifon, then the play button. The machine is meant to record up to five hours of conversation, with a microphone that is sensitive enough to pick up both sides of a phone conversation. To preserve the battery and recording capacity, it automatically stops after twenty seconds of silence. I can tell by a small meter display that the total length of recorded material is less than half an hour. Barry truly is a loner.

I sit through a string of mundane conversations. One with his mother. Another with his physician and a third with his pharmacist. On the fourth call, I hit pay dirt.

I hear Barry Davis's voice answering an incoming call. "Hello."

"Hello, Barry. Remember me?" A male voice, no trace of an accent.

"Don't be sarcastic. Of course I remember you. How could I forget? What do you want?"

"You know what I want. Is it ready? We had a deal."

"I haven't forgotten. I'm working on it. Didn't I specifically tell you not to call me here?"

"I don't think you want to use that tone with me, Barry."

"Is that a threat? You've got to be joking. One word with the man and I could have you eliminated. You think they would let you cook the goose that laid the golden egg? Just how dumb do you think I am that you could threaten me? How dumb are you is the real question. Don't call me again. Ever. I may have it for you Wednesday night. I will see you, as we agreed."

And with that, the call ends with a very loud disconnect.

I ponder the call for a minute. Who could be on the other end of that call? And what deal was Barry to deliver on? This could be a middleman who gets information from Barry and passes it on to the Swedish embassy. But, if that is the case, as Barry pointed out, he doesn't sound too smart. Why risk calling Barry at home? Too risky, I would think. But, perhaps this man is being pressured in turn, and in his desperation thought he could speed things up by strong-arming Barry. I have to hand it to Barry Davis. He sure didn't act like someone who could be intimidated.

I decide that the only way to get to the bottom of this is to keep closer tabs on Barry, starting tonight. I make my way to the Masonic Lodge and park in the shadows where I can watch the doorway. Barry should be easy to spot given his arthritic limp and cane.

I'm not disappointed. Shortly after ten p.m. the doors open and a procession of men file out. I spot Barry as he exits. I notice he's carrying something, and I'm certain he didn't have anything in his possession when he left his apartment. As the other men hurry away from the meeting hall towards their cars, Barry slowly descends the stairs. A moment later a black sedan pulls up. It's not a taxi. Barry gets in and I follow them at a discreet distance. They arrive back at Barry's apartment and he gets out of the vehicle. His hands are empty. Whatever he took out of the Masonic Lodge is now in the car.

Should I follow Barry, or should I follow the car? Unless I plan to confront Barry, there is no point in following him into his apartment, so I decide to follow the car. As I'm driving I think about what to do. Should I try to stop the car somehow and find out who the driver is, and even better what's in the package? If I find documents from Eldorado, we have our man and his accomplice. But, that course of action seems reckless. What if the package is just some innocuous material dealing with Masonic Lodge business? I decide the safest course of action is to keep tailing the sedan and see where that leads.

We are now heading west along Highway Two. We've already gone through Newtonville, Newcastle and Bowmanville. It's been almost forty-five minutes since we left Port Hope and I'm starting to worry that I may run out of petrol. Finally, the car stops outside of a run-down duplex in Courtice. A dark-haired driver gets out, retrieves the package from the back seat of the sedan, and heads towards a door at the west end of the building. I exit my truck and follow, sticking to the shadows. I edge my way along the side of the building and notice a lit window about half way towards the backyard. I duck under the window's edge and slowly peek above it. I can see a dimly lit table with the driver and another pale, blonde man looking at the package on the table. They seem quite pleased. The blonde man pats the driver on the back, and hands him a tumbler of whiskey. They clink glasses, sit down and Blondie begins to pry apart the package with a blade. Once he's peeled back the wrapping from one end of the package, he pours the contents onto the table.

I see a number of small bundles wrapped in wax paper, tied with string. Clearly not documents. But, I'm curious. What am I seeing here? Blondie disappears into the next room and returns with a shoebox. He reaches into the box and pulls out a small Bunsen burner, a spoon, a syringe, and a rubber band. I know now what I'm looking at. I'm looking at Barry Davis's side business. He has a lab set up somewhere (possibly in the Masonic Lodge) and, using his chemist expertise, he's making heroin. I don't need to watch what the men will be doing. I leave quietly and memorize the address.

This likely eliminates Barry Davis as the source of leaked information from Eldorado. He's a criminal, but not my criminal. So, by process of elimination, my man would be Paul Greer. But, I have no proof of this. I've yet to see him make any move that would implicate him. What if Finegan's list of suspects is off? What if none of the four men on his list is passing secrets, and there is another, unsuspected, who is getting away with it?

As I make my way back home I think about my next move. The party at Massey's Batterwood estate isn't until Saturday night, three days from now. I suppose I could tail Greer and maybe even try to watch his movements at work. The other, more attractive possibility, is to revisit Nadia Mironov. Perhaps she knows something.

Thursday morning arrives and I conduct my daily check of my drop box. This time there is a familiar encoded message: 'Glider Molson 9pm'. I am to meet someone at the Ganny at ten p.m. After work I return home, change, have a light dinner with Agnes, then at 9:30 make my way to the Ganny. As I sip beer at the bar and make small talk with Lainey, I keep an eye on the entrance. At ten, a shadow crosses the threshold, and a man briefly glances at me and puts his left index finger to the side of his nose, then turns and exits the bar. This is my signal. I quickly finish my beer, pay my bill and head for the door. As I'm walking towards my car, a black Buick pulls up beside me, the driver's window rolled down. It's Intrepid.

"Get in."

I do as I'm told. This must be something big for him to come here and see me in person.

"Well, Glider, you've stirred up a bit of a hornets' nest this time."

"A pleasure to see you too, Intrepid."

"Well, I am happy to see you, but this isn't a social call. We have a delicate situation to handle and I'm afraid you're going to be the one to handle it."

"Aren't I already handling a delicate situation for the Twenty Committee?"

"Yes. And that is one of the reasons you will be handling this one as well. The two situations are related."

"Go on then. Tell me."

"You had asked us to find out information about a young woman named Nadia Mironov. I assume you asked as you suspected her as a conduit for one of our primary suspects?"

"Yes. She has been sleeping with Paul Greer. I thought maybe she was a go-between for Greer and the Swedish embassy."

"Well, it appears you may be right. She is a go-between. But, not between Greer and the Swedish embassy. It appears she is sending encoded information. What that information might be and to whom she is sending it, we have not established. Our friends at Blechley have yet to decipher the message, but they can confirm without a doubt it isn't being sent to the Nazis. We have our suspicions who the recipient is though."

"Let me guess. She is sending information to our allies, the Soviet Union."

"That is our suspicion, yes."

"Hmm. So, I can see the dilemma. I assume

we've left our friends and allies out of our plans to build an atomic bomb. They may be a bit miffed if they knew about it. Meanwhile, we can't continue to let this foreign agent operate unmolested, regardless of whether they are friend or foe. Is that about the gist of it?"

"You do catch on quickly. Yes, that is the crux of the matter."

"So, what would you have me do then?"

"You will do nothing for now. If the Soviets are receiving the same information that we plan to send to the Nazis via Greer, then we will know for sure that she's a Soviet operative. We will also know that the Soviets are also trying to develop an atomic bomb. If the Soviets find out that we double-crossed Greer into passing along bad information, we can claim we had no knowledge of the Greer/Mironov connection."

"You said 'for now.' What happens after we've turned Greer?"

"That will depend on what happens between you and Mironov. If we confirm that Greer is our connection to the Swedes, we'll let this play out. Then we'll move to disconnect Greer and Mironov. How that disconnection is made will be up to you, but, ultimately, we'd like to retain the services of Miss Mironov."

"By 'up to me' you mean I'll have two

choices: one, turn her to an asset, or two… eliminate her."

"There may be other options, but right now I don't know what they are."

We drive in silence. He drops me off a block from the Ganny and I retrieve my car and slowly drive home. Saturday can't come soon enough.

CHAPTER 11
THE SWEDISH CONNECTION

I arrive at Batterwood early to touch base with Massey again and to meet his niece. She's a sweet, if docile young lady, named Nancy. As we chat, she seems happy to have an escort for the event, and equally happy that it has been arranged by her uncle. I get the impression she is extremely shy.

As guests start to arrive, we lose ourselves in the crowd. Slowly Nancy gravitates towards her mother and her aunt, who are keeping to the periphery of the room. This makes it easy for me to watch for the Swedish ambassador, Svend Salming.

He arrives as cocktails are being served, and is greeted by Massey himself. There are other dignitaries, including representatives from the US, Swiss, French, English and Portuguese embassies. Most have made the trip from their Toronto consulate offices and are staying overnight. They've grouped themselves in one corner, while the scions of Canadian agriculture and manufacturing, including Paul Greer, have grouped themselves in another. The women who have accompanied these men divide into similar groupings. I catch myself scanning the women, wondering if Greer has had the brazenness to bring along his mistress, the lovely Miss Mironov. I'm mildly crestfallen to see he has not.

Finally, at around 9 p.m., the man himself arrives. Massey catches my eye and a silent signal is exchanged between the two of us. Massey greets C.D. Howe and after a few moments he taps his champagne glass to get the attention of the crowd.

"Ladies and gentlemen, may I have your attention, please."

After a smattering of murmurs, the room goes silent and Massey continues. "I'm sure many of you know the man to my right, but for those of you who do not, may I introduce Mister C.D. Howe. C.D. is too modest to admit it, but he is the man behind the wheel of our wartime economy, which, I must say, is smashing all expectations. It is not boastful to say that Canada has come to the aid of Great Britain in a most spectacular way, and much of that is due to C.D.'s efforts in marshalling the best, the brightest, and the most productive that this country has to offer."

The group applauds loudly, and there are cheers all around.

"C.D., will you say a few words?"

C.D. Howe is not an imposing figure, and yet, there is something about the man: his forbearance, his sharp inquisitive eyes. He completely captures our attention, then speaks.

"I thank you, Vincent, for those kind words. I will keep this brief. As most of you are aware, Canada's economy is going through the roof. Our biggest constraint is that we are limited by the number of ships we can build, buy, or borrow, to ship exports. Of course, many of our exports must, by necessity, go towards the war effort. However, we still have a surplus of many products that we think you, as allies and non-combatants, might find beneficial. Similarly, you might find an opportunity to open up an import channel into Canada for items that we need. Tonight, I hope you can mingle, discuss possible trade, and in the coming months and perhaps years, grow trade between our countries. One thing though: don't make a deal without me. I might get in hot water with the War Office."

The last comment produces some laughter and serves as an ice breaker, and we follow C.D.'s lead and raise our glasses in a toast. I see men crossing the floor, introducing themselves to Mr. Howe.

I watch Greer and Salming carefully. They seem to be deliberately avoiding each other. But in their desire to deflect suspicion, to this trained eye they only ramp up suspicion. But, suspicion isn't proof. I make small talk with some of the other guests, and do my best to keep Massey's niece Nancy engaged, while keeping one eye on Greer.

It's nearing midnight, and the gathering is starting to break up. Finally, Svend Salming approaches Greer. They appear to exchange pleasantries, and Greer says loud enough for anyone close by to hear, "I must take my leave, and it appears that I am blocked in. Is that your blue Chevrolet sedan near the end of the drive, Mr. Salming? I believe you are staying overnight?"

"Yes, I am staying the night and that is my car. I will move it out of your way."

Greer bids adieu to our host, retrieves his coat from the cloak room, and the two men head to the door and outside.

I excuse myself from Nancy's company and head to the large picture window facing the parking area. It's a bright moon-lit night, with a blanket of snow reflecting the moon. I can see the two men talking as they make their way to their automobiles. I get a good look at Salming's face. He seems irritated, shaking his head and frowning. Greer shrugs and holds his hands out to his side in a 'what can I do?' gesture. Clearly, they are no longer making small talk. They reach Greer's car and he unlocks the trunk. He reaches in and brings out a file folder, which he hands over to Salming. As they part, there is no handshake. The exchange is quick and all too orchestrated not to have been pre-arranged. I notice that there is no car blocking Greer's. It seems this may be the smoking gun I am looking for.

Salming strides to his car, unlocks it, and climbs into the back seat. A moment later he exits, locks the car and heads back towards the house. He is no longer carrying the file folder.

I find Massey, catch his eye, and beckon him to follow me. We duck into the pantry.

"I'm afraid I need to impose on you again, Mr. Massey."

"Of course. What can I do for you?"

"I'd like to stay the night, if you can accommodate me."

"That's it? It's nothing at all; I'll have a room made up for you. May I ask why?"

"Let's just say I have some nocturnal prowling to do. On that note, one other thing. I understand Salming is staying the night. Can you make sure he is accommodated at the back of your residence, and as far away from the driveway as possible? And that my room is at the front of your home, preferably on the main floor?"

"We have no bedrooms on the main floor but I can have the sofa in my den made up for you if you would find that suitable. I'll put Salming in the rear bedroom on the top floor. Sounds like you are on to something."

"I am, thanks to you. And a sofa would be just fine."

"Happy to be of service. I'll just speak to my housekeeper to have the rooms made up."

It's three a.m. I'm relieved to be prowling at night instead of tossing and turning in bed, awaiting my latest nightmares. Massey, true to his word, has had me set up in his den, while Salming is on the top floor facing the backyard and the forested area to the southwest. I tiptoe out of the room and silently glide out the front door and make my way towards Salming's blue sedan. It is locked, but I efficiently open it with my lock picks. I quickly duck in and quietly close the door, then search the back seat where I find what I'm looking for. I open Salming's briefcase and there is a plain vanilla folder.

I open the folder and see that the contents are slim; only two pages in total. I briefly scan the material. Highly technical, and also very specific, they describe a process called thermal diffusion. Chemicals, temperatures, and pressure figures are highlighted. In the margin on the second page, I see a handwritten note. It reads 'Tube construct???".

Before returning the document to the folder, I place the pages on top of the briefcase and snap photos with my Minox camera. Yet another device that my Abwehr counterparts would be familiar with, the Minox camera is easy to conceal and a must-have for any would-be spook. I will share these images with Home Office, which will hopefully direct us in determining how best to derail the Nazi efforts to build their bomb. It will also afford me the evidence I need to confront the traitor, now confirmed as Paul Greer

CHAPTER 12
LOOSE ENDS

I'm the first one to rise at Batterwood, and after scribbling a brief note of thanks to my host, apologizing for my early departure and explaining my desire to attend church with my grandparents, I'm on my way. I drop the film from my camera at the drop box, along with an encrypted note explaining what I witnessed.

Back at my room in the Schock residence, I change clothes and ready myself for church service. As I'm about to leave, I hear Agnes downstairs. I haven't forgotten my promise to her, but haven't been able to decide on a course of action yet. I decide to go downstairs and reassure her.

"Good morning, Agnes. How have you been?"

"I'm fine, thank you Marcus. Thankfully,

Darren Wilson hasn't visited me since our last episode."

"Yes, about that… I haven't forgotten my promise to you. I will find a way to deal with Wilson and his threats."

"I believe you. And I promise, I won't say anything about your past to anyone about this. Not if you don't want me to."

"Yes, it's best to keep all of this to ourselves for now. But, don't worry, it will all be sorted out soon. You have my word." I leave her, noting a strained smile on her face.

After church, I say my farewells to my grandparents and promise to be at the farm for dinner. There is another loose end I decide to deal with today.

Barry Davis isn't a threat to national security. That said, I can't let him and his drug peddling friends continue to operate, knowing he could inadvertently or intentionally divulge sensitive information. I decide on what I believe will be a simple yet effective way of handling the situation. I make my way to the phone booth located in the Queen's Hotel in downtown Port Hope.

"Hello, operator… can you connect me with the Ontario Provincial Police please?" I wait for my call to be connected.

"Ontario Provincial Police, Staff Sergeant Pierce speaking. How may I help you?"

"Hello Staff Sergeant Pierce. I have information that may in fact help you."

"Yes, sir. Please continue."

"Tell me, have you noticed an uptick in the illegal sale and use of illicit drugs in Southern Ontario recently?"

"As a matter of fact, we have."

"I have a name and two addresses for you." I tell him of the home I followed Barry's outlaw friend to in Courtice and, with some reluctance, Barry's name and address.

"Barry Davis is a chemist. He is producing illegal drugs, although where he does that and where he procures his raw materials is not known to me. As for the address in Courtice, I believe this is the distribution hub."

"This is all very interesting information, sir, but it will be difficult for me to obtain a warrant without knowing your name and exactly how you came about this information."

"I'm sorry sir, but I can't divulge either of those things. But, what I can say is that if you follow Mr. Davis on Wednesday evenings he will eventually lead you to his accomplices and all the evidence you need to make arrests. Goodbye."

I hang up without hearing a response. I hope that this will be enough to put the wheels of justice in motion. At any rate, I've done enough to clear my conscience.

I head back to the family farm. I need some time to think about Agnes and her sticky situation with Wilson. My options are somewhat limited. I could wait until my official mission is complete, then confront Wilson before I move on. But, that wouldn't necessarily be a lasting solution. He may continue blackmailing Agnes once I'm gone. I may also inadvertently cause him to panic, which could lead him to tell both Laslo Miclos and Darius Szalsis of Ronald Schock's past. Removing Wilson isn't an option. While I loathe the man, I can't become some kind of reckless vigilante, dispensing justice as I see fit. Home Office would definitely not approve.

I decide the best way to handle it is to remove Wilson's leverage. If Miclos and Szalsis are removed, or at least compromised in such a way that they aren't a danger to anyone, then Wilson and his threats will become hollow.

Darius Szalsis is an unrepentant fascist, an extremist who subscribes to racist ideas. He should be easy to neutralize. I can use these hostile traits against him.

Laslo Miclos is another problem altogether. His hatred of the fascist Hungarian Angel Cross Party and the old Austrian-Hungarian Empire cannot necessarily be used against him; not when we are fighting a war against fascist Germany and her annexed ally Austria. But, perhaps his extremism can be coaxed into action, especially if it is stoked by pride.

First, I need more information about both men. Then I will act.

I duck out on my lunch hour on Monday to visit my drop box at the train station. There is a single slip of paper inside that reads one word: 'stasis'.

This is our simple code word for 'hold tight… don't act until further notice'. I'm left with the uneasy feeling that Paul Greer may pass along more information while we are in stasis mode, however, I'm also aware that this order is likely coming from either Finegan or Intrepid, so I'm confident they have things under control. This also gives me time to deal with Szalsis and Miclos.

I head to the Port Hope Public Library, and I find what I'm looking for in the census information kept on file.

Darius Szalsis arrived in Port Hope via Hungary in 1936. He's a thirty-nine year old bachelor.

Laslo Miclos is a more recent arrival. He came to Port Hope via Serbia after being in a Swiss refugee camp in 1941 to -42. He's only just turned thirty and is, like Szalsis, a bachelor.

I next consult the phone book and find addresses for both men.

That night, I decide to visit Szalsis's modest bungalow on Elgin Street first. I find the house apparently unoccupied: no car outside and no lights inside. I use my trusty locksmith kit to gain entry to the back door. What I find inside is incriminating to say the least. Szalsis's basement is a virtual shrine to our enemy, Nazi Germany. I see a portrait of the German mad man on the wall. I see a stylized Hungarian flag that includes something resembling a combination of a swastika and a traffic sign. This must be the Arrow Cross Party emblem. I see other war memorabilia, including swords, bayonets, and helmets. Then, jackpot: I find a locked cabinet. I pick the lock and behold a stash of weapons: rifles, handguns, ammunition.

I've seen enough. Time to check on our friend Miclos.

I locate his house on Young Street and see that it's lit up. Seeing no one nearby, I discreetly walk alongside the house and peer through a shaded window. Unlike Szalsis, Miclos is at home – in his kitchen and pouring himself a whiskey. This gives me the opportunity to see the man in person... he's a healthy looking young man, looks to be about five-nine, of average build, with thick black hair, dark brown eyes, bushy brow and a five o'clock shadow.

This is all I need to see of Miclos to make up my mind. I return to my room and pen two letters for Home Office.

One is regarding Szalsis. The bottom line for him is that he will be in an internment camp in forty-eight hours.

The other letter is for Miclos's future: he will find a draft notice in his mailbox with instructions to report to the Canadian Army barracks in Prince Edward County by the following Wednesday.

I congratulate myself on my handiwork. I have no doubt that Home Office will make these things happen. They may even find more of a hornets' nest when they investigate Szalsis, but for now, I believe I've found a way to cease Wilson's blackmail of Agnes.

It's now time to refocus on Greer, but, in stasis, I can't act until advised. Perhaps in the interim I can revisit Nadia Mironov, at least that is the name we know her by. I have not been instructed to look in on her, but I haven't been instructed not to either.

CHAPTER 13
NADIA REVEALED

It's Wednesday and my workday has just ended. As usual, I make my way to the train station and check my drop box. There is an envelope. I slip it into my breast pocket, and head out on foot for my apartment.

I don't get far when, out of the corner of my eye, I notice motion. The kind of motion I've been trained to recognize: I'm being tailed. Evasive maneuvering isn't easy in a small town like Port Hope; there isn't enough foot traffic, no bustling market places, or cars to dodge to make it challenging for the pursuer. That said, it also makes it difficult for the pursuer to remain inconspicuous. But I have extensive training in this regard so I don't panic. I feign unawareness; I don't let on that I've spotted them. I use my small town knowledge to my advantage, taking my usual way home up Pine Street, plotting where I might make my escape. Or do I need to be more daring? If so, where to ambush my pursuer.

I decide on the latter course of action. I must find out if my mission has been compromised. I decide on my spot. There is a pie shaped lot on the right where Pine Street intersects with Walton Street. It is a sharp, hedgerow-lined corner, and if I turn onto Walton and duck behind the hedgerow, I can wait until they make the turn, then I have them. Even though Walton is a fairly busy street, the lighting is meagre and I believe I can accomplish this manoeuvre surreptitiously. I dare not look back, so I'm not sure if they are still in pursuit, but, I must assume they are, and I prepare. I take the right turn and pivot into the hedgerow, crouching behind the bushes and pulling out the switch blade that I keep hidden in my left boot. In less than fifteen seconds I hear a footfall, and see a shadow pass a few feet from my face. Quickly, and silently, I step out from the hedge behind my pursuer, position the blade at their throat with my right hand and apply a choke hold covering their mouth with my left hand.

"Don't budge an inch or I'll sever your artery and you'll bleed out in less than three minutes, understand?"

An affirmative head nod. To my slight surprise, I realize it is a woman I am dealing with.

In a low but menacing voice, I advise her. "I am going to remove my hand from your mouth. No shouting, or you're dead. You're going to tell me who you are and who you work for."

I slowly remove my hand from my pursuer's mouth, subtly applying more pressure on the knife to her neck in case she gets any ideas. I pull her behind the hedgerow, out of sight from passing cars.

"It is me… Nadia. Nadia Mironov. Do not hurt me… we are allies."

"Allies?! Really? Is this what allies do… spy on their friends? You said you were from Minsk, Belarus. Who are you really? And don't bother lying any more. I know your name isn't Nadia Mironov."

"And I know you are not a plumber. So we are even. Can we go someplace where we can properly talk? I do not think standing here like this will help either of us."

She has a point, and I can't help but admire how calmly she has reacted to this sudden turn of events. "All right. I'm going to let you go, but I warn you. If you try to run, you won't get far."

"Da. I will not run."

I disengage her from the choke hold, but continue brandishing my knife. She turns to face me, and once again I'm struck by her beauty. But I won't be distracted.

"Okay, cross Walton and keep walking down Pine Street. I will be directly behind you."

She does as she's told. I direct her to the staircase that leads to my private entrance at Schock's.

"This is where you live," she says matter-of-factly.

"Yes, it is. So, you've been following me for a while then?"

We are in my room now. She's removed her coat, as have I. The switch blade has been closed, but I'm still clutching it, perhaps even harder now than I had been. Clearly, despite the fact I spotted her tonight, this woman has been trained in surveillance. She's a pro. Which means, like myself, she's been trained to disable any threat.

"Yes, I have watched you now off and on, even since you visited my flat. You realize of course how clumsy that was? Did you really think I believed your story, or not bother to check with my landlord? I knew you were lying immediately."

"Well, perhaps if you weren't suspicious by nature and trained to spot lies, I would have got away with my 'clumsy' attempt to find out who Greer was meeting. So, now we come to the crux of the matter. Why Greer? What is going on between him and you? And, as I asked before, what is your real name, and who do you work for?"

There is little hesitation and I get the impression that she is relieved to be caught. "Okay. I am ready to tell you my story. But, can we sit down?

And, maybe you have something strong to drink?"

She says this as she appraises my room. There is something about this woman. Her beauty and strength, added to an air of intrigue, draws me to her. But I still cannot trust her. I'm leery of letting my guard down, yet I realize that if I'm going to get information from her I'd much rather do it over a drink in my room, as opposed to a Camp X interrogation chamber.

"I've got some rye whiskey. Sorry, no vodka."

"I have grown accustomed to your Canadian whiskey. Yes, please. Two fingers, neat."

I pour our drinks and motion her to the sofa. "All right, you said you'd cooperate. I'm all ears."

"I am going to start at the beginning."

"That's always a good place to start." I smirk at my own joke. She looks at me deadpan. I realize that I'm acting like a condescending jerk. "Sorry, go on."

"First off, I did not lie about where I am from. I do come from Minsk in Belarus. But, to say this, it is not enough. You must understand Belarus in order to understand me and why I do what I am doing."

I look into her eyes. I believe there is a

sincere desire to be understood. An almost desperate look. I find myself drawn in. "Okay, tell me. I'm not going anywhere."

"I will tell you what it is like to be Belarus. To be Belarus is to be in the center of a sand storm. The desert dunes shifting under your feet. And you are often blinded by the storm, or seeing things that do not exist, like a mirage. First, you are Polish. Then, you are German. Then you are Russian. Sometimes you are even Latvian or Lithuanian. After the Great World War, we Belarus were split into two parts: one part in the west, dominated by the Poles; the other in the east, dominated by the Imperial Russians. Many Belarus were not satisfied being second class citizens in their own country. My grandfather, like many others, fought hard for a Belarus Republic, but the Poles and the Imperial Russians each dominated and in the end signed the Treaty of Riga that spit our country in two. My grandfather was killed in 1923; I was just six years old. In the east, the Imperial Russians began to outlaw our language and sent many people to the outer regions of Asia, like Siberia. In the west, the Polish veterans who had fought Russians on our soil moved in and displaced many more people. They too banned our language. I was in the east, so I learned in Russian schools. But my mother and father taught me how to speak Belarus and, although Russia made anything other than their Russian Orthodox religion forbidden, we prayed in our Greek Orthodox way at night.

"Then the Soviet Russians came and expelled the Poles. For a brief period, the Soviets let us open our schools to teach in Belarussian language. Although, they also deported many Jews. But that only lasted a few years. The Germans turned on the Soviets and broke their pact that had so cynically divided Poland, and, once again Minsk was overrun. The Germans were brutal. They did not only deport Jews, they killed them. They burnt entire villages to the ground and rounded up people for slave labour. My father left us and joined the resistance, and he was killed. Many who disliked the Soviets suddenly looked to them for hope. They supplied our resistance movement. This is when I was recruited. I had looked to join the resistance, but it turned out the person I was to meet was not from the resistance. He was NKVD. You are familiar with NKVD?"

I'm struck by the similarity of our circumstances: both of us wanting to fight the enemy and ending up being recruited by intelligence services. I answer her question, "Yes, the NKVD's purpose is to protect the state security of the Soviet Union, but I believe they operate using somewhat nefarious methods. I had guessed as much: you are NKVD."

"Da. Yes, I am."

"Go on."

"I was trained by the NKVD to go behind enemy lines and set up communications with the resistance groups in Belarus, Poland and the Baltic. At least, that is what they told me."

Again, I can relate entirely to this, including

the anomaly of her being here. "And yet… here you are in Canada."

"Da. I came to Canada, with help from the NKVD, as a Polish refugee. Once here, I was to contact the Soviet consulate in Toronto. There, they gave me new papers, identifying me as Nadia Mironov. My real name is Sofia Novartov, but, that is of no consequence now. There is nobody alive to remember that name. My mother and father were killed by the Nazis during the German occupation."

I see tears welling up in her eyes. I can tell this story is both draining and bitter for her. The war has been hard on her, as it has for been for so many of us. But, we need to press on.

"So, tell me, Nadia… why did the NKVD send you to Canada? I think I know the answer, but I need to hear it from you."

"Very well, I will tell you. But first, I need you to know something else. I do not spy for the Soviets out of patriotic love, or idealist yearning for all to be living in a perfect socialist state. I do it because I hate the fascists and what they did to my parents. We Belarus, we are so used to war, to occupation, to being displaced, imprisoned. We have been bullied for centuries; the Soviets are no better than other occupiers. But, only the Nazis are responsible for my parents' death. As the Turkish say, 'the enemy of my enemy is my friend'."

The tears she shed earlier are now replaced

with a look of determination and strength. It is clear that Nadia is not a shrinking violet, and equally clear that, like me, she can push down her emotions when she needs to.

"I understand. But what do you do when your friend sends you to spy on another friend? Why Canada? And why Paul Greer?"

"I do not like this. I do not like spying on our allies. And, honestly, I do not trust the Soviets. But what choice do I have? Once you are an asset of the NKVD there is little choice but to do as you are told. To do otherwise is to face liquidation. So, I did as I was told. I was told to be nice to Paul Greer, to get close to him, then to find out about his factory in Port Hope. Find out what they do there and how they do it."

"And how has your mission gone so far?"

"I have been able to make progress on my mission, but Paul Greer is a pig. An unscrupulous, greedy pig."

I can see pain and loathing etched across her face. I don't need to ask to know that she had to sleep with Greer to get what she wanted. It revolts and angers me in a way that it shouldn't. One of the prime directives of my training is to remain detached. I pause, but then continue my questioning.

"So tell me, how do you get the information from Greer, and how do you send it to your handlers?"

She balks. "You are asking too much of me now. Why should I tell you more?"

I have to tread carefully here. This has progressed much faster than I, Finegan or Intrepid would have imagined. I'm not sure Nadia realizes that there is only one option for her that holds a possibility of ending well. She agrees to be an asset and to help us sabotage the Soviet's quest to build an atomic bomb, or... or what? She could have an accident. Or, she could be an embarrassment to her Soviet handlers who could claim she was not acting on their behalf. Then she would likely be sent to a Siberian gulag or simply shot as a traitor. I decide to lay cards on the table.

"Look, Nadia, we can either come to an agreement, or you can stonewall. If you decide not to cooperate, there is no chance this will end well for you. Whereas, if you cooperate with me, I can give you an opportunity to hurt the Soviets, the Germans, and Paul Greer. And, I guarantee they will never know you were involved. In fact, the Soviets won't even be able to disclose they were hurt, because that would be an admission of this mission you are on. That would not be good for allied relations."

Of course, there is another way out for Nadia. I think back to my training and the cyanide capsule I had with me the entire time I was behind enemy lines in Norway. But, surely she sees these circumstances are different.

I watch as her mind processes. Again, I'm struck by just how beautiful she looks, and right now, perhaps a bit fragile. But, I know, based on her story, she is anything but fragile. I believe she has it in her to take her own life. I have to be cognisant of what that would mean to my mission. How would Paul Greer react? Would he suspect foul play? Would he or his handlers suspect he'd been compromised? Nadia still hasn't told me how she obtains information from the pig Greer. Maybe he knows as much about her as I do. I suddenly realize that if this is the case, she's playing me and I've just exposed myself to a potential double cross.

"Nadia. What's it going to be? Do you want to cooperate with our side? Or… do you want to end up being one of the casualties?"

She stands and turns away from me and remains silent for what seems like a long while, then turns back. Her face is tight, controlled. "All right. I do not see an alternative. But, how do I know you will not use me, then… dispose of me?"

"You don't know for sure. You'll just have to trust me. As I'm trusting you not to tell your handlers about me." I stand and walk towards the door. "I'll be in touch." I watch from my window as Nadia descends the stairway into the dark, cold night. We are now bound to each other, her fate and mine inextricably linked. It is not trust at this point that bonds us, but the certainty that if either of us is compromised, the other will also be in grave danger.

CHAPTER 14
FALLOUT

I have mixed feelings when I read the news in the Port Hope Evening Guide. The headline reads:

'Local Man Barry Davis Found Murdered in Drug Lab Apartment, Courtice Man Charged'.

A local man, Mr. Barry Davis, a chemist at Eldorado Mining and Refining, was found murdered in his apartment on Ontario Street in Port Hope on Wednesday evening. The apartment housed an illegal drug lab, with a quantity of heroin found bound in small packages.

Port Hope Town Police, acting on information from the Ontario Provincial Police from an anonymous telephone tip, were following Mr. Davis when he made contact with a man outside of the Masonic Temple. Police witnessed what appeared to be an argument, then both men got into a vehicle and drove to Davis's apartment on Ontario Street, with police following and conducting surveillance. One male left the apartment thirty minutes later, and officers knocked on the door, but getting no response they broke the door down and found Davis lying in a pool of blood, with his throat slit. Officers subsequently arrested Mr. Gary Reynolds at his home in Courtice, where they found a quantity of heroin as well as a knife believed to be the murder weapon. Mr. Reynolds, a known felon, has been arrested and charged with murder and possession of heroin. If convicted, Reynolds is expected to spend a lengthy sentence in prison.

Having lunch in the cafeteria, I'm trying to process this information. I can't help but feel some guilt. If I hadn't have put the cops onto Davis and the house in Courtice, maybe his murder would not have happened. It is an uncomfortable thought. During my time in Norway there were many men killed, both foe and friend. Some by my own hand, some at my command… and some were just unlucky combatants. In the heat of action I'd always remained detached, and only in recent months have I started to confront the psychological scars that remind me of those actions. But, somehow this feels different. For whatever reason Davis may have been turned into a criminal, just as I'm going to turn Greer into an asset. Barry Davis wasn't my eventual target for this mission, yet I went out of my way to destroy his freedom.

My thoughts are interrupted by Darren Wilson, who I know still holds a grudge from our run-in at the Schock residence. I see him coming my way.

"If it isn't the high and mighty Marcus

Andersen. Here, slumming with us factory hands in the cafeteria."

A small group of men one table over are trying to ignore this confrontation, but are failing badly.

I can't resist a smart-ass retort, "And just what can I do for you, Mr. Wilson? Do you need another lesson in manners?"

"I won't give you the satisfaction, Andersen. Besides, you've already done enough."

"What is that supposed to mean?"

He approaches and lowers his voice. "It means you've already come between me and Schock. It means I know what you did. Because of you, Randal and Agnes won't have anything to do with me."

I scoff at this. "Perhaps the Schocks have found you to be wanting. That has nothing to do with me."

"Ah, but I think it does. Let's just say that there are mutual acquaintances that I shared with the Schocks who have suddenly disappeared. And this happened right after we had our little conversation at the Schock residence. Curious, isn't it?"

"Oh, you mean the conversation when I punched your lights out? That one?" Something about Wilson brings out the worst in me, but his alluding to the disappearances of Miclos and Szalsis should put me on alert.

"And the follow-up conversation you had with Agnes. Yeah, that one. What I don't understand is how one man is able to pull so many strings. Maybe you'd like to tell me. Or, maybe it's your little secret. You know, I love secrets. They offer so many possibilities."

Wilson leaves with a satisfied grin on his face. I mull this over. Obviously he knows something. How much he knows is anyone's guess. I will have to speak with Agnes. She doesn't know the specifics of how I got rid of Miclos and Szalsis, but does Wilson have the brains to put two and two together? More importantly, could he blow my cover?

I know Wilson's game. If he thinks he has something on me, he will attempt blackmail. Threatening an agent in His Majesty's Secret Service is not a good idea, but, if I was to tell him that, or even allude to it, then I would in no uncertain terms be blowing my cover. Can I possibly ward him off without him ending up dead? I need time to think. Again, I'm struck by how different this is from my time behind enemy lines. At that time it was simple: kill or be killed. Now, I can't help but feel once again I've set this man on a course that could decide his fate… and if his fate is death it will be on my hands.

I work the remainder of my day with these thoughts churning in my head. I need to act fast, but

I can't think of a way out of this that doesn't end with Wilson as collateral damage. And, I still haven't had a discussion yet with Finegan or Intrepid about how to deal with Nadia. I believe she can be an asset, but what if they don't agree? There could be more blood on my hands. An involuntary shudder travels down my spine.

As I check my drop box, my mind clears. I've been summoned again. I'm to go to the Ganny this evening and await further instruction. I hope that this will be my opportunity to bring Finegan and Intrepid up to speed, as I don't relish the thought of trying to explain all of this through coded messages.

I hurry home, change out of my work clothes and rehearse what I'm going to say to my Twenty Committee controllers. On my way to the Ganny, I'm more cautious than usual, looking for tails and hidden threats. Has Wilson already talked to some of Szalsis's fascist friends? Maybe he's already blown my cover and it's just a matter of time before they come at me. Or, maybe my trust in Nadia is ill-founded. Maybe I spooked her into looking for help and I'm now a target of one of our supposed ally's secret service, the Soviet NKDV. Regardless of the threat, real or imagined, I know I have to be more careful now. I've come too far for this mission to be derailed. Strangely, I feel very at home being careful. It saddens me a little that paranoia has become my normal state of mind.

I enter the Ganny and see the regulars seated at the bar. Schock is there, chatting with Lainey.

Wilson is nowhere to be seen. A few other Eldorado workers nod in my direction, then return to their beers. I get Lainey's attention and order a draft. She seems relieved to be clear of Schock. After a few minutes, I notice a couple of burly men huddled at a corner table. One catches my eye, nods and heads towards the door. Before I can acknowledge, the second man repeats this dance. Sending two men? This must be urgent, or, like me, my handlers are beginning to suspect I may have been somehow compromised.

I quickly down my draft beer, pay Lainey and head out. As I head towards my car, one of the men from the bar steps out from behind a parked car and starts following me. After several more paces the other man emerges from a parked car and holds the back passenger door open. He clearly wants me to get in the car. Should I? Something seems off. But, I did get summoned. Perhaps my imagination, or paranoia, is getting the best of me. I climb into the car, with my shadow right behind me. Neither Intrepid nor Finegan is in the car. We speed off heading out of town; it's a familiar route, we're likely heading to the abandoned farm.

We arrive, with neither of my escorts nor me saying a word. I get out of the car and head towards the barn and its converted granary. There, finally, I'm greeted with a familiar sight: Intrepid and Finegan bundled in warm clothing, huddled around the small wood burning stove.

Intrepid spots me, "Ah, our guest of honour

has arrived. Do have a seat, Glider. We need to talk."

That is an understatement. I do as I'm told and pull up a chair close to the fire. "Good evening Intrepid, Finegan. I must say, that was quite the subtle escort tonight."

Finegan chuckles lightly. "Yes, those lads do tend to make an impression. Junior members of our Twenty Committee, I asked them not to engage in any conversation, really to protect you, and them. I hope they didn't put you off too much; you may see more of them. We believe we are nearing the end of the mission and we want to make sure nothing goes wrong."

By that I believe Finegan is implying that the purpose of my two brawny escorts is to run interference and look after any potential threats. My pride is a bit wounded that he would think I need some type of bodyguard, but I realize that this isn't personal. I quickly push those prideful thoughts aside.

"I admit I did hesitate before getting into the car. But, I have to say, they followed your orders impeccably. Not a word was uttered the entire trip here."

Intrepid speaks. "Just as well you saved your vocal cords; we have much to discuss. Starting with Greer and how we're going to handle him. Finegan, please fill Glider in."

"Yes, certainly. Glider, we took a look at the information you passed along. It is legit. It comes from Eldorado and contains exactly the type of information we want to keep out of the Abwehr's filthy hands. Furthermore, it is also worrisome because with this level of detail it would seem to indicate they are more advanced in their work than we had first thought. Wouldn't you concur, Intrepid?"

"Yes. Yes, it would seem to indicate that." Intrepid looks worn. I've not known him to look so worried.

Finegan continues, "Tell me, Glider, did you take a close look at the documents when you photographed them?"

"I would not say close, but I did look at them, yes."

"And, did you notice the handwriting in the margin?"

"Yes. It certainly aroused my curiosity. On the second page, it said 'tube construct', with question marks."

Finegan has a tight smile. "Not much gets by you, Glider. Yes, that intrigued us too. Turns out, we can use this if it means what we think it means." He pauses, apparently collecting his thoughts.

I'm dying of curiosity, so I ask, "Care to fill me in? What do you think it means, and how can we use it?" Often questions like this are answered with a very curt, 'You don't need to know.' But, as I look over at Intrepid, I see him give a slight nod to Finegan.

Finegan finally continues. "The process to enrich uranium is known as thermal diffusion. This is basically a high pressure, high heat process used to separate uranium into its smallest elements. With me so far?"

I nod. "Of course. Remember, I'm an engineering grad."

"Ah, right. Sorry if I'm belabouring. Anyhow, the 'tubes' that this margin note refers to are our key to mitigating the Nazis' progress. They need to be constructed in such a way as to withstand the thermal diffusion process… otherwise… things will go sideways in a hurry."

Finegan continues, beginning to describe the plan. "What we will do is switch Greer's tube construct plans with plans that we've drawn up. We will leave those in your drop box."

I ask the obvious question, "But, how will we know when to make the switch? I've not yet turned Greer, and I can't monitor everything he's taking out of the …"

Intrepid intercepts. "This is where things may get dicey, Glider. We think we can get a two for one here, if you follow. We need Nadia Mironov. We think she can make the switch, and, while she's at it, send the same edited information to her Soviet handlers. The other thing to consider here is that we don't know what the NKVD or Abwehr have on each other. Suppose either or both sides are compromised… someone might spot an anomaly. It suits our plans that they both see the same thing; it's consistent and shouldn't raise any red flags, despite the… shall we say… unfortunate outcomes." Intrepid's eyes twinkle with the look of school boy mischief. He's enjoying this, despite the stakes.

This was not the original plan. I was to find the source of our leak to the Swedish embassy, then hopefully turn them into an asset. The new plan leaves Paul Greer operating as an enemy agent, and also puts Nadia squarely in the middle of this entire operation.

I voice my concerns. "But, we still don't know if we can trust Nadia. Also, we don't know how she's intercepting information from Greer, nor do we know how she sends it on to her handler in the NKVD. Wouldn't it just be easier to turn Greer?"

Intrepid looks at me and I can tell he's already had this discussion, if not with Finegan than certainly in his mind.

"I've thought of the pros and cons. My concern is Greer himself. I'm not saying we can't turn him in the future, but, at this point, I don't believe he has the stomach for it. I think he'd crack under pressure and do something stupid. Also, he's proven that he's greedy. Can you ever really trust a man who is mainly motivated by money? As for Nadia... well, yes, you are right, there are still some unknowns around logistics. But, what we do know is that she has acted for many months now as an operative. That takes a cool head, as you well know. Also, unlike Greer, she isn't doing this for the money. We've done more research on her background. We know about her family in Belarus. She hates the Germans and only hates the Soviets to a slightly lesser degree. I think she'd jump at the chance to get back at both."

This confirms the story Nadia has related to me of her time and family in Belarus. I relay this to Intrepid and Finegan, and this seems to reaffirm their plan and makes all of us just a little more sure of her. We are all in agreement. Only one more thing to add.

"So, I assume you will want me to work through the logistics with Nadia?"

Finegan replies, "Yes. The fewer hands we have in this, the better."

I nod in agreement (and in truth I'm secretly delighted). It appears our meeting is over, but then Intrepid looks at me, a cloud of worry passing over him. He wants to say something.

"Glider, have you read the news from England lately?"

"Yes, I have."

"So, you are aware of the Nazis' new weapon… the missiles they've been sending from across the channel? These missiles… they are unstoppable. The best we can do is send misinformation about their accuracy and hope that we draw them off target. Do you realize the significance of this?"

"Yes, I do. If one of these missiles was to be armed with an atomic weapon…"

The rest is left unsaid. The Nazis had been perfecting these missile strikes since September, despite D-Day landings in June. Their range was beyond anything that we could imagine, or match, with missiles still hitting targets in England despite the Germans being pushed east, almost back to their own borders. If those delivery systems were operating to send atomic bombs, success on the battlefield wouldn't matter. London would be obliterated and we'd have no choice but to negotiate for peace. A peace dictated by the dangerous lunatic, Hitler.

CHPATER 15
THE TURN

It's Thursday evening. As usual, I'm spending some time with the lads at the Ganny, discussing things from work, the war, sporting events, and women. I've come to appreciate these little bull sessions and the comradery they provide, despite the false pretenses. I realize after being home all these months just how much 'home' really means to me. But, I can't stay long. Tonight is the night that I have in mind to work with Nadia to develop a plan.

I find myself using the term 'working with Nadia' as opposed to 'turning Nadia'. It happened unconsciously, but I can't deny how appealing the thought is. I'm holding to my hope that she doesn't feel coerced, but I need to be prepared for any possibility.

I arrive in Newcastle around eight p.m. It's a cold, overcast night with very limited visibility. There are no pedestrians, and no traffic to speak of. I decide to keep driving past her cul-de-sac and park a couple of blocks down the street. As I draw nearer to her address, I see apartment 101B is lit up from the inside, so I am fairly certain that she is at home. How should I play this? It's not like Greer to visit Thursday nights, so it's likely he's not there. As I walk to her place, I decide I will peek inside first. I silently creep up to her living room window, and peering inside, I see that she is sitting alone, reading a book. I knock on her door.

She opens the door a crack, keeping the chain lock on, peers outside and, on seeing me, raises her eyebrows, steps back and quickly opens the door just wide enough for me to step inside.

"It is bold of you to arrive like this. Were you followed?"

"No, I wasn't. Besides, who would follow me?"

"There are spies everywhere. Why do you think you are immune from that? Canadians are naïve."

"Perhaps. But, we are also diligent people. I've not been followed by any spies since coming back from Europe, except you. And you're not an enemy... at least I don't think you are."

"You sound sure of that. Can I be sure of you?"

"Absolutely. Have you thought about what we discussed last time we met?"

"Yes, I have. And, as I said last time, I believe you leave me no choice."

"That's true, but, in the interim, things could have happened. Things that are dangerous to me or to you. But, that didn't happen, so I hope maybe now we can trust each other."

"Perhaps. So, you have a plan. Tell me."

"Actually, I need you to tell me a few things first. First off: how do you obtain information from Greer, and how do you get that information to your handlers?"

This is the point of no return. Once she divulges this information, she is essentially turned. I'm pleasantly surprised to see that she has no hesitation. She looks determined, with her eyes slightly narrowed and her lips sealed in a thin line. When she speaks, it's with a cool detachment.

"The pig Greer usually comes to my apartment twice a week. Saturday and either Tuesday or Wednesday. Occasionally Sunday too, if he decides he is doing his duty so God will not be offended if he 'works' on the holy day. When he first starting coming, he always carried a briefcase, presumably because there is something important in it. That makes me think maybe I can find what I'm looking for. And… I find it. He has documents. I can tell; they are from the place he works.

His habits are always the same. We drink; we have a nice heavy dinner; we dance. He drinks much whiskey – I encourage him – and then he passes out on the sofa. While he is asleep, I take his briefcase into the bedroom, close the door, and quickly photograph the contents."

Nadia pauses, goes to her bedroom and returns with a small camera. "I take the undeveloped film from the camera and mail it to a post office box in Ottawa."

"Okay. It is likely a drop box for the Soviet embassy. What happens when he wakes up?"

Nadia visibly shudders. An expression of disgust, anger, and angst clouds her features. I can deduce what then transpires between them, and I realize I've touched a very raw nerve. I feel embarrassed for both of us.

"Never mind, Nadia, I guess that's not relevant."

Nadia's face turns from disgust to defiance. "What I do then with Greer is not relevant, but it is necessary. I must keep him interested."

I move on, quickly changing the topic. "Okay. The plan is simple. I will provide you with documents prepared by our forgers. When Greer visits you, you will exchange his documents with these forgeries. This will also be the version of information that you photograph and pass on to NKVD."

"But how will we know that Greer has not already studied the information and will notice the discrepancy?"

"We can't be certain, but we believe that is a risk we have to take."

"'Yes, 'you' are taking a risk, but 'I' am taking a very large risk. If he thinks his documents were tampered with and tells his handlers, or he panics and runs, I will be the one who they come for."

"That is true. But I promise I will make sure you are protected."

"Will you? Even if your plan fails? Or, will you leave me for some NKVD wet team, or just as bad, you will have me deported?"

"If the plan fails, the fascists will know not to trust any information coming to them from Greer, so that will stall their efforts. As for the Soviets, if they somehow discover that the Nazis have abandoned Greer, they will no doubt recall you from the field. So, we'd need to weigh options. We would never deport you, Nadia. But let's not get ahead of ourselves. Succeed or fail, you are now an asset to us and that comes with as much protection as we can provide, depending on the mission."

I leave it open-ended, but the implications are now clear to her. She has crossed a line that can never be uncrossed. She is now a double agent. It is difficult to read her expression. Is that resignation, relief, or, dare I surmise, is she actually showing traces of relief, or even happiness? I don't question her on this, but as I get up to leave and she escorts me to the door, her hand rests on my back. I turn to look at her and we say our farewells. If I'm not mistaken, there is the merest hint of a smile.

"I'll be in touch just as soon as I have the documents that I want you to use for our switch; hopefully this Friday. I can also brief you on what to look for in his documents. For our odds to increase, we want the real documents and the fake documents to cover the same topics. Does Friday work for you?"

"I look forward to it. Yes, Friday is fine."

I leave feeling like I've just made a date for the prom. It's an odd sensation, given the stakes involved. But, I can't help it, nor do I want to suppress this feeling which is such a contrast to the stress and strain I've felt for so long. Butterflies have replaced anxiety.

CHAPTER 16
THE SWITCH

Friday night I drive through a snow storm to Nadia's apartment after picking up the falsified documents from my drop box. I've reviewed the documents and, from the many internal specifications I've read during the course of my cover job at Eldorado, they look flawless. The same paper and letter head, the same font, the same technical documentation reference system (a series of numbers and letters used for filing and security clearance referencing). It dawns on me that Intrepid must have other assets within the Eldorado hierarchy, otherwise, how would this document be so flawlessly manufactured?

Impulsively, I stop at the local florist and purchase a poinsettia. I arrive at Nadia's apartment and, like the previous night, I see that the interior light is on. I drive the neighbourhood and I'm happy that Greer's car is nowhere in sight. She must be home and, hopefully, alone. This is yet another test of our mutual trust. If she had any thoughts of double-crossing me, this would be the time to do it. I peer into her partially shaded window. I see her comfortably lounging on her sofa, reading a book. A good sign that she's alone. I knock tentatively at her door.

She greets me with a smile and I quickly slip in through the barely opened doorway.

"I am glad you are here tonight. Greer has called me and he plans to drop by tomorrow evening."

"Perfect. I've brought these and want to go through them with you." I hand her the file folder from under my winter coat.

"And I see you have something else too. It's lovely!" I hand her the poinsettia, remove my coat and galoshes, and we make our way to her living room.

"Would you like something to drink? Tea, coffee... maybe something stronger? I have whiskey."

"A whiskey neat would be excellent, thank you."

I seat myself on the sofa, in front of the coffee table where Nadia has placed the file folder. She makes her way to a small bar cart, pours two whiskeys and returns to the sofa. I've fanned out the twenty or so pages of the document on the table for us to review. I notice her brow furrow.

"Don't worry, you don't have to memorize all the content. I want to show you the important parts, in case only a partial swap is possible, or there is the possibility of contradictory documentation that you need to remove."

This seems to calm her. She sits beside me on the sofa. I'm temporarily mesmerized by her fragrance and the heat radiating from her body so close to mine. As her unofficial handler, the temptation to use that leverage flickers on the edge of my consciousness, but is quickly extinguished. If we are to trust each other, I must not let my baser instincts lead me into something that I know I would be ashamed of. I cannot deny the attraction, but, I remind myself that I'm not the type of man that Greer is. I won't use my power, money or influence to cajole this women into an intimate relationship. Maybe my charm, good looks and intelligence will win her over, I joke to myself.

I can see the look of puzzlement on her face as she tries to interpret my stillness, and quickly snap out of my revelry to begin preparing her for the document exchange.

"Do you see this reference number at the top of each page?"

"Yes."

"Think of it as an encoded message to the reader that gives them the idea of the general area being covered, the specific topic within that general field, and the intended audience and security clearance for the document. Are you with me so far?"

"Yes. I have seen these numbers before in other documents and I do have a general understanding of how to de-cypher them."

"Good. Then you will understand that we're looking for documentation that covers the general area of liquid thermal diffusion, the specific topic of plant construction and, of course, this would only be seen by plant engineers who have the highest clearance." I point to the various fragments of the document reference code to highlight their meanings.

"I see, and I know what to look for, except for the reference to plant construction. Do you know what values would be embedded in this reference code?"

"I don't know if the encoding is accurate, but I believe it is. That's what you can confirm when you see the documents that Greer brings tomorrow. If the general topic and audience as denoted in this document matches the ones you see, then the coding reference for plant construction may not be as critical, but, ideally the entire reference should be identical. It will be a judgement call on your part whether to proceed with the swap or not."

Her emerald green eyes widen at this. I can

tell she is surprised, but also pleased, that we have put our faith in her on this.

"Now, as to the content, it is likely that there will be two things to look for to confirm we are making the switch at the appropriate time. One, we fully expect that there will be a schematic showing what the final product should look like. Here, this is what we want to see."

I pass her a page from the content that shows a tube or column, roughly forty feet in height, with measurements of various component parts.

"In addition, there will be a detailed description of how these tubes or columns are made. You need to look for a combination of a nickel inner lining with a copper outer coating, along with the type of pressure that they are built to withstand. This is the most critical part. If the document that Greer brings does not have these things – the schematic and the detailed description of the construction of these tubes or columns – then do not make the switch, even if the document reference numbers look similar. Do you understand?"

"Yes, perfectly. And, these documents that you bring with you tonight... I am to photograph them and send to my Soviet post office box in Ottawa, correct?"

I can see the look of trepidation on her face and note a slight tremble in her hand holding the document. It is one thing to trip up the Germans but quite another to trip up her Soviet spy masters. Without thinking, I place my hand on hers.

"Yes… you can photograph these now if you like… but don't pass them along unless you also make the switch with Greer's material."

There is a demure look down, at my hand on hers. She raises her eyes to mine. I read a look of desperation there. A look of someone who feels utterly and totally alone. I long to comfort her, but I know that now is not the time. I have to keep our relationship strictly professional. I disengage my hand, but offer words of encouragement.

"Nadia, you know what to do. And you are right to do it. The Soviets are a convenient ally to us in the fight against the axis powers, but, you know as I do that they can't be trusted. When peace comes, it would be an enormous tragedy if the Soviets dominate Europe, and with your help and a bit of luck we can make sure that that doesn't happen."

She nods her head. I can tell she is committed, but I also know the decision weighs heavily on her.

I retreat from the sofa, and retrieve my coat and other winter gear, preparing to leave. She escorts me to the door and as I turn to say goodbye, she leans toward me, tilts her head up, and brushes her lips against my cheek.

"Thank you," she whispers.

I stand back, again fending off the urge to take her in my arms. "Thanks for what? It is me who should be thanking you."

"Thank you for trusting me. I won't let you down."

"I know. I know you won't. Goodnight, Nadia… and rest assured, you have my word that I will do everything in my power to make sure you are safe once this is all over."

"I believe you. I do… Goodnight, Marcus."

As I make my way down the street to my truck deep in thought I realize that, for possibly the first time, I truly trust her. I sense she sees the good in this cause and that she believes I won't betray her. We are now truly committed to each other in this mission. And, I admit to myself, commitment for me runs deeper than the mission. I think I'm falling in love with this woman. That realization shakes me. I know that in this line of work, it can complicate things and lead to sometimes fatal mistakes. And yet, I can't deny it, and, I also can't deny that I like the feeling. It seems to go hand in hand with the comfort I've been allowing myself to experience little by little as my stay at home has continued. Perhaps one feeling feeds off the other. I can't let myself be overwhelmed; at least not yet. There is still so much important work to do.

As I drive towards home I suddenly come

into a snow squall, which heightens my awareness. It is then that I notice through the blowing snow that there are headlights following at a discreet distance. Is it paranoia on my part to think that I'm being followed? I continue to carefully make my way back to Port Hope, with the vehicle tailing me all the way. Given the weather conditions, we appear to be the only vehicles on the road tonight, which elevates my suspicions. Did this vehicle follow me all the way to Newcastle? Did the occupants watch as I entered Nadia's apartment? Have I put her in danger, recklessly meeting her at her home without picking up a tail? Or, perhaps even more disturbing, were they waiting at Nadia's and have tailed me from there?

My paranoia is slightly dispelled when, as I turn onto Pine Street on my way to my room at the Schock residence, my potential tail peels off and turns right onto South Street. We are, after all, on the cusp of the holiday season and it is Friday night, when people are generally more active and sociable. Nonetheless, I plan to be extra cautious, and I also plan on being very close to Nadia's apartment tomorrow evening when the document switch is hopefully made. Nothing must stop this plan from working; and nobody is going to threaten Nadia's safety. As I circle the streets and finally make my way to my room I am fairly confident that there was no tail.

After a night's sleep, where I dreamt of Nadia instead of my usual hellish visions, Saturday arrives with a bluster. The snowstorm that blew in from Lake Ontario continues and has so far dumped half a foot of very wet, heavy snow.

I dress and make my way downstairs. The Schocks are engrossed in the paper, but both Randal and Agnes greet me warmly. Although not part of our original agreement, they usually insist I join them for Saturday breakfast, where we all enjoy reading the Port Hope Evening Guide over hot coffee, toast, bacon and eggs.

We discuss the snowstorm and they inform me that tree limbs are down and electricity is out in some parts of Port Hope. I briefly excuse myself, and am relieved that I'm able to contact my grandparents and to find that they have power and are well provisioned to whether the storm. They invite me for dinner that evening, but, given my mission, I make an excuse but also promise I will be by early on Christmas Eve.

Randal places the front section of the paper in front of me. "Did you read this? The Nazis fired more of those rockets at London on Thursday. Most of them missed their target, but not all. It is very sad to see the English having to deal with a second blitz. It's also hard to believe these missiles even exist. Imagine being hundreds of miles away and still being able to cause death and destruction."

If only he knew. "Yes, the Nazis won't give up. It's clear this war won't end until the allies are marching in Berlin. Hopefully that happens soon."

There is a brief moment of silence while we

all think of what the end of the war will mean. For me, personally, I can't even contemplate it. This war is ending, we are all sure of that, and perhaps it will end very soon. But, on the horizon, all I can see are more clouds gathering. Nadia and her Soviet handlers are reminders that the world isn't a safe place, even in times of so-called peace and cooperation.

After breakfast I help Randal shovel the snow off their driveway and sidewalk. The snow is heavy, and, with a drop in temperature, it is freezing fast, making for difficult work. Soon Randal is spending more time leaning on his shovel than actually shovelling. But I truly don't mind the distraction of this physical labour. After our work is done, we retire to the living room. Agnes is busy with some sewing, but at her father's request she fetches us both a late-morning warm brandy.

"I suppose you have plans for Christmas, Marcus?" Randal enquires.

"Yes, I'll be going to my grandparents the day after next and spending the holidays there."

"Well then, perhaps an early Christmas toast is in order. Merry Christmas, and let's hope 1945 sees the end of this war."

We down our brandies and, before I can refuse, Agnes has refilled both of our glasses. I notice that she has poured a small one for herself as well.

"And here's to old friends and new possibilities," she toasts.

I smile politely and sip my brandy, but I can't help but feel uncomfortable about Agnes and her toast. It seems that ever since I got that swine Darren Wilson out of her life, she's been very attentive where I'm concerned. Maybe too attentive. I get the impression that she is looking for new possibilities with this 'old friend'. If that's the case, soon I will have to disappoint her... but, not before my mission is complete.

Pleasantly warmed by the brandy, but feeling the need to clear my head, I decide to take a walk in the winter wonderland and grab a bite to eat at the Queen's Hotel downtown… I'm not in the mood for the Ganny. I feel my nerves on edge as I anticipate the evening's plan, and the risk to Nadia. When I return to my room later that afternoon I feel confident that I haven't been followed but I still feel an uneasiness.

I trudge up the stairs to my room to prepare for the evening. First, I strip down and put on my thermal underwear and double wool socks. I can't say how many nights in Norway I would have frozen to death without these undergarments. Next, I select my black wool pants along with the black knit turtleneck, both also designed to help keep me warm and camouflaged during dark winter nights. My black combat boots complete the ensemble. Next, I select my weapons. I retrieve the shoulder holster and Smith and Wesson M1917 six shooter from the hidden compartment I created in the floorboards under the bed. I purchased this pistol before the war started, but I am certainly happy to have it now. I prefer the .45 to our standard issue 32 calibre Walther PPK, but I am not about to leave that weapon behind. I slip on my heavy naval wool jacket and conceal the PPK in the right pocket. In case things get up close and personal, I also carry my switch blade, which I slip into a sleeve in my boot. I pull on my black knit cap and black leather gloves, and head out my private door. It's December 22, winter solstice, the shortest day of the year, and sun sets early at 5:15 p.m. It's unseasonably cold and the sun is already low in the horizon. By the time I get to Newcastle, darkness will have set in. As I make my way to my vehicle it briefly crosses my mind that black may not be the best camouflage colour with all of this snow, but it's too late to buy a new outfit now.

Before heading out of town, I check my drop box. There is a coded message. It's a warning. It seems that I wasn't being paranoid last night leaving Nadia's; there was someone watching me. This will be the last message I receive from this location and someone will reach out to me with further instructions. I feel a knot building in my stomach at the realization that Nadia might be in real danger, or worse.

I head out on Highway Two, on extra alert should someone be following me. After ten minutes on this straight road, I'm certain that nobody is. As I enter Newcastle's town limits, I slow down. I decide to continue on King Avenue past Baldwin (Nadia's cul-de-sac apartment is off Baldwin). I can hide the pickup near the creek just west of Baldwin, then circle back on foot. Now familiar with the neighbourhood, I know I can position myself in such a way that I can see anyone approaching Nadia's, whether they be on foot or in a car. I have a spot in mind, and, as I make my way down Baldwin, I pivot into the backyards that run the length of the cul-de-sac across the street from Nadia's apartment. Her neighbour across the street has a garage, separate from the main house. I duck in through the garage's back entry, which is fortuitously unlocked, and make my way to the large garage door. The decorative diamond shaped windows are small, but are at eye level and offer a perfect view once I remove the accumulated dust. The garage offers the bonus of cutting the wind, which has picked up since I left Port Hope, causing snow drifts to form in front of the garage and on the driveway. I'm now in place, and, as my eyes adjust, I take better stock of my surroundings. The garage contains very little, but, I can see that a car is usually parked in here based on the wet tire tracks and an oil stain about three quarters down the length of concrete floor. The walls include some gardening tools hung by hooks, along with a push mower shoved against the back wall. The absence of a car worries me somewhat, but, I decide, if push comes to shove, it will be easy to make a quick exit out the back door before whoever wants to park their car, if they can even make their way to the garage door and open it.

I settle in, expecting Greer to arrive at Nadia's soon. I'm not disappointed. I see his car approaching, and, unlike the other time I followed him here, he decides to park right in front of Nadia's place… perhaps the snow and wind have caused him to be less discreet. He lifts his bulk from the driver's side door, and I'm relieved when he reaches into the back seat and brings out his briefcase. He waddles up the walkway and the stairs that lead to Nadia's door and knocks. I catch a glimpse of Nadia as she opens the door and my heart skips a beat. She looks as lovely as ever, and I can't help but feel a stab of jealously and a deep-seated loathing as Greer enters her apartment. However, I tamp those feelings down as the awareness sets in that this could be the night we've all been waiting for.

Based on my conversation with Nadia, I know this evening could be quite long. I'm grateful for being prepared for this cold weather clothing wise, but realize I should have thought of bringing a thermos of hot coffee. And perhaps a sandwich for later. I spot a folded lawn chair hanging from the garage wall and consider settling in, but decide it's best if I keep up a continuous surveillance out the diamond windows. I promised Nadia I would do all I could do to keep her safe.

After about an hour, I spot headlights turning onto the cul-de-sac. I see a dark sedan drive by, then circle back and park a couple of houses down on my side of the street. A man emerges from the car and I immediately recognize him: Darren Wilson.

My mind races. Could this be who followed me last night? What is he doing here now? I quickly stop thinking and start acting. Regardless of why he's here, I can't afford to have him interrupt the proceedings, intentionally or unintentionally. I race to the back of the garage and quickly retrace my steps back to Baldwin Street. As I peer around the corner, I see Wilson cautiously moving towards Greer's car. I follow quickly and quietly behind him; the wind and snow together with the darkness offering cover.

Wilson is bent over, scrubbing dirt off the license plate as I place the muzzle of my Smith and Wesson against his temple and pull back the hammer.

"Not a word, Wilson, or I will blow your brains out. Understood?"

"What the hell?" he manages to stammer before I pistol whip him.

"Last warning. One more word and you're a dead man. Now, get up and raise your hands... or should I say hand?" I can be a cruel bastard when I need to be.

Wilson gets up slowly, raising his right hand and the stump of his left hand. His eyes slowly take in the scene and as he recognizes me, they turn to a look of pure hatred mixed liberally with fear. I take the Walther PPK from my jacket pocket, and holster my Smith and Wesson.

"The PPK is easier to conceal, Wilson, but make no mistake, it can still put a hole in your head. Now, I'm going to keep this in my right hand, cocked and ready. If you decide to run, I won't hesitate. Are we clear?"

"Sure, Andersen. Whatever you say."

"Okay. Start walking to your car."

As we are walking, my mind is racing. What can I do with him? I guess I need to find out what he knows before I make a decision.

"All right, Wilson, hand me the keys, then get in the driver's seat."

He does as he's told and I walk around the front of the car and get in the passenger seat, the gun pointed at Wilson the entire time. I hand him back the keys.

"Drive… back east on Highway Two, then we'll go north on Burnham Street at Cobourg. Got it?" I need to figure out what to do with him and a plan is starting to form in my head.

"Sure, I got it. What do you have in mind, Andersen? A little picnic on Rice Lake?"

"Very funny, Wilson. Now, while we're driving we're going to have a little chat. What were you doing back there?"

I can see he's starting to get uncomfortable. His eyes keep darting from the road to the gun I've got leveled at his chest. Despite the cold, small beads of perspiration start to form on his brow.

"You know, that really is none of your business."

"Well, I'm making it my business. Start talking, or this is not going to end well for you. I don't think you know what kind of trouble you've gotten yourself into."

"Oh, really? Why would you be the one to shoot me over a little love triangle? Ridiculous. It's not you that will be paying me anyway. Last I heard, you're not making the big bucks, or married with kids. But, I have to admit, I was quite surprised to see you visiting her last night. She sure gets around, that one."

Wilson just confirmed my suspicion. He's the tail who followed me back to Port Hope last night. I'm both relieved and angered by this news. "Ah, so that's what this is about. You're onto another blackmail scheme. This time Greer is your target, is that it? Going to get him to cough up some money or you'll squeal on him to his wife?"

"Can't put nothing by you, eh? Now that we're being so open with each other, maybe you can explain where you came from and why you have that gun? Don't you and Greer try to avoid each other when you're visiting that dame? Or, hey, maybe you were there to get rid of Greer?"

"That's enough! You stupid fool. You have no idea what kind of trouble you're in. Now just shut up and keep driving."

We ride in silence for another half hour. Wilson doesn't know anything about my mission, but, he's the only one who can connect me with Nadia. I can't let him dig deeper or somehow tip off Greer to my relationship with Nadia. I need to find a solution to this problem and somehow I'm drawn to Rice Lake like a nail to a magnet.

As we approach the intersection of Burnham Road North and County Road Nine, I know I must make a decision, and soon. If we continue heading north, in less than two miles we'll come to the little village of Gore's Landing, where the road terminates at the edge of Rice Lake as a boat launch. My decision is made. I steel myself.

"Keep going straight, Wilson. Slowly. I'll tell you when to stop."

He does as he's told. We begin a steep incline down, heading into the village. With about two hundred yards to go before we hit the end of the road, I tell him to stop the car and put it in park.

"All right, now what, Andersen? You're going to leave me here? In the middle of nowhere? You really haven't thought this through, have you? You know, the second you drive away I'm going to be knocking on someone's door and calling the cops. Why don't you put the gun down? I told you… I'm not going after you. Greer is the big fish here."

I see he's getting desperate, and desperate

people do desperate things. I don't hesitate. With an arching motion I swing the pistol at his head, hard. He's knocked unconscious and falls sideways to rest his head against the driver side window.

The snow continues to swirl around us. Visibility is bad, which works out well for me. I get out of the car, and move to the driver's side. Wilson slumps as I open his door. I push him towards the passenger side, and open the driver side window. I arrange his feet so they are not touching any pedals, then reach for the shifter on the steering wheel column and shift into neutral. Straightening out the steering wheel, I step back and close the door as the car starts to slowly roll downhill towards the lake. I give it a hard push then stand back and watch as it gathers momentum.

The ice on Rice Lake is barely formed, a layer of two inches would be my guess for this time of year and this unusually cold December. It certainly will not hold the weight of a vehicle. I continue to watch with morbid fascination as the car picks up speed travelling straight down the hill. I estimate it hits the waterline doing about twenty miles an hour. With its momentum it slides out onto the frozen lake three quarters the length of the car, then the ice cracks, and breaks. The car travels a few more feet, and as it slowly sinks the tail lights flicker, then short out. Finally, from my vantage point, there is no trace of the vehicle… just a hole in the ice where it went through. With these cold temperatures, by morning a new layer of ice will have formed, and all traces of Wilson and his car will be consumed by the murky depths of Rice Lake.

I wipe the tears from my eyes. Again, I'm surprised by the emotions I'm feeling. Back in Norway I would have almost celebrated something like this. Any threat to the mission must be eliminated. But here, on home turf, having to kill a man… a fellow Canadian no less. It just seems so cruel.

As I start walking back up the hill, south towards County Road Nine, I shake off my introspective thoughts and start to think again as an agent. An agent with a mission to complete that could save hundreds of thousands, if not millions, of lives. Wilson's life is insignificant in the balance, I try to tell myself.

I need to find some transportation back to Newcastle and fast. I want to be there to make sure Greer leaves and Nadia is safe.

Less than a mile into my journey I spot a small home on the right side of the road, with a late model Chevy coupe in the driveway. I walk to the car and am relieved to see it is unlocked, as I didn't think to bring my lock picks. Hotwiring the car takes less than half a minute. I'm on the road in no time, retracing the route I'd just driven with Wilson. Wilson, that bloody fool.

On my way back to Newcastle I begin to experience a familiar feeling: a grim determination that I truly haven't felt since that night, now so distant, in Norway. I've done things, in the name of

King and country, but, now more than ever, I'm seeing this war is even bigger than that. It's about the future of humanity. It's about keeping the power to destroy civilizations out of the hands of mad men. Nobody can stand in my way or sway me from my course, and if it means unscrupulous men like Wilson, Davis and maybe even Greer ending up as collateral damage, so be it. But, what of Nadia? Would I make the same call if her life were in the balance?

I'm lost in these thoughts as I enter the town limits of Newcastle. Perhaps I'm rationalizing, but I can't dwell on it. I ditch the borrowed car at a drug store parking lot on King Street, several blocks east of Nadia's place and begin my walk, staying in the shadows. I see headlights approaching and duck into a darkened doorway to avoid being seen. As it passes by, I recognize at once that it's Greer's car. I check my wrist watch and I'm surprised to see it's almost midnight.

I hasten my pace and reach Nadia's doorway. My fear for her safety, and the mission, sends adrenaline rushing through my veins and is overwhelming. I don't have to knock; she must have been looking for me. She opens the door quickly and, as I enter, she throws her arms around me and kisses me. Her warm, soft lips part and we have a long languishing kiss.

"Nadia… I'm…"

"I am so glad that is over." She whispers as we part.

"Do not speak now. Come with me."

She leads me to her bedroom. I feel elated that she is safe, and know from her actions that the mission is safe, too. We start silently removing each other's clothes. I wrap my arms around her as she leads me to her bed. We make frantic love, and then sweet long, lazy love, like we've known each other for years instead of weeks, our bodies anticipating and wanting.

CHAPTER 17
TRIPLE CROSS

I wake up before dawn the next morning. Nadia is lying across my left arm, her head nestled on my bicep and shoulder. I try, unsuccessfully, to extricate myself without waking her. She tilts her head up towards me. "I'm sorry, I didn't mean to wake you."

"Do not be sorry. I am glad you woke me. We must talk. But first..." She leans over, kisses me, smiles. "This is how I would like to wake up, with you in the morning. And if we had more time, we would make love again. But I know, you cannot stay."

I smile at her. "You sure aren't making this easy." I extract myself from the bed and start to gather my clothes and get dressed. "I need the details of how it went last night. Is that what you want to tell me?"

"Yes. And then there is something else…"

From the seriousness on her face I can sense something is wrong, but don't press her yet.

"First, the switch. It went exactly as planned. Here." She reaches under the bed and grabs a sheaf of paper. "I will make coffee while you take a look at those." She puts on her bathrobe and I again admire her casual sensuality.

I follow her to the kitchen and spread the papers out on the table. I begin by looking at the document reference numbers, mentally comparing them to the ones on the forged papers. They look almost identical to the numbers we used in the forgeries. It's unlikely anyone will notice the differences, especially Greer. Next, I find the schematic. Again, almost identical. Lastly, the technical specifications. All the same subject matter is covered, albeit in slightly different orders with slightly different wordings, and, most importantly, slightly different gauges and materials for the tubes. I'm satisfied that only someone extremely familiar with the content of these original documents would recognize the differences in our forgeries.

I smile as Nadia brings me a coffee. "It's perfect." I say. "You're perfect. Now… what else do we need to discuss? Is something wrong?"

She steps back. I can see concern on her face, and then tears forming in her eyes. "Yes. I am afraid something is wrong. Yesterday I was contacted.

They told me that my mission here is very close to completion and that, once finished I was to take the train to Ottawa and go to the embassy. I am afraid they are going to reassign me. Where? To do what? I do not know." At this, she breaks down, covering her face and quietly weeping.

I take her in my arms. "Nadia, please, don't cry. Remember, I promised that you won't be deported."

"Yes. I know, you did promise me that. But this is not deportation, this is something entirely different. How can you stop this?"

She has a point. If I try to stop her from leaving, then her controller will look at her as a defector or possibly even a traitor. This could mean her information is tainted. Our mission could be sunk.

Our eyes meet. I can't hide my thoughts any better than she can. But, I can't let her believe there is no hope.

"Nadia, I'm going to talk to my handlers. They might be able to help us here. Maybe they can make us both disappear; I don't know… but don't worry about this. Do you hear me? Just play along for now and I promise I will come back as soon as I can with this all sorted out. Okay?"

"Yes, okay. I will play along. But I must send this film as soon as possible… so we don't have much time."

"I know. But, lucky for us postal delivery is sometimes very sporadic at Christmas time. Don't send it right away. Wait until I tell you, okay?"

"All right. I trust you, Marcus. And… I love you. Last night with you sleeping beside me was the first time in years I've not had nightmares about Belarus, my parents… everything. You make me feel safe and loved."

I'm caught off guard. The words reverberate in my head and make me dizzy. What I thought was childish imagining on my part is turning into reality. "I love you too. I do. You and I… we have much more in common than I thought possible. I will do everything in my power to keep you here and safe."

We embrace and kiss one more time, I gather up the documents, then I head out to retrieve my truck and make my way back to Port Hope.

Once in town, I scribble an encoded note 'switch made', with another remark, 'need to talk', and leave it in my drop box with the original Eldorado documents. Although I was told to no longer use this box I really don't have a choice since they have not yet communicated an alternative. I fill the rest of my Sunday afternoon chatting with Randal and Agnes, getting caught up on town gossip and local news. Thoughts of Nadia are never far from my mind, and I find myself worrying about her, and pondering a possible future together.

When I check my drop box later that evening, I find my notes and the technical documents are gone, but nothing has been left in their place. Happy that my message was received, I'm uncertain how further communication will be handled.

The next day, Christmas Eve day, I head to work. It's a half day, where not much is actually accomplished. People socialize, exchange small gifts and make plans to meet up after work or during the Christmas holidays; a two week plant shutdown. There is some murmuring of Wilson not appearing for work, but most people put it down to either 'unsociable behaviour' or 'a Christmas hangover' from too much drink over the weekend. I check my drop box one more time on the way home (still nothing) before heading to the Ganny to have a quick pint before heading to my grandparents.

My grandparents take my comings and goings in stride now. As we get caught up, I tell them that I have a woman friend, and although we are not yet serious, I have strong feelings for her. I deflect all of their questions deftly, telling them I will introduce her to them, but she isn't able to meet them until the New Year. She is very busy and can't disengage from her holiday obligations to visit just yet. She wants to keep her identify secret until then… a surprise for them. This starts them speculating.

"Is it that girl Lainey who works at the Ganaraska Hotel? I have seen the way she looks at you…" my grandfather guesses.

"Or is it that girl who lives with her father in the Schock house where you are staying... Agnes? Right?" my grandmother guesses.

"No. Neither of them. And I'm not going to tell you, I promised her. Besides, you don't know her."

I can see the look of bemused puzzlement on their faces. I must admit, this story I've told them is taking on a life of its own and I'm rather enjoying it. Perhaps soon, hopefully, they can actually meet Nadia.

I drive into town and check my drop box again Christmas Day. I'm relieved to find an encrypted message, informing me to rendezvous at the barn on Boxing Day at six a.m. This is odd, since all of our previous meetings have been late at night. Nonetheless, I am anxious to meet, as I believe they are.

At dinner that night, I enjoy the holiday spirit with my grandparents. They have invited the neighbours who live to the west of us, the Brooks. They have an orchard, and also some acreage where they grow tobacco. I'm friendly with their two sons, Burritt and Doug, but both are deployed and won't be home for Christmas. We toast to their health and to the end of the war, which is looking more and more likely to happen in the near future. Of course, none of them know of the Nazi's potential to prolong and possibly win the war with a new and terrifying weapon. Talk revolves around country gossip, and my mysterious new girlfriend. Everyone seems happy and the mood is light. At around eleven I beg off, telling them I have an early morning rendezvous with my mystery woman. They all laugh and I can hear them speculating more as I alight the stairs.

Once again, I'm up hours before dawn. I quickly dress, put on my outdoor wear and head out for my rendezvous. The roads are deserted, since most have the day off and are still sleeping. I get to the barn slightly early, but as I approach the grain bin/command post, I smell coffee and hear voices.

"Ah, Glider, you are early. Please, come, sit, have a coffee."

"Coffee; thank God. I can use it."

I pour myself a generous mug and take a seat at the table. As usual, Finegan and Intrepid are already seated, but I notice two others lurking in the shadows.

"Glider, these two are Hunter and Gatherer. Don't be alarmed, they are here strictly for security. We aren't broadening the mission."

I wonder about the meaning behind their two names but put those thoughts aside as we exchange nods.

Intrepid continues. "Congratulations are in order. It appears our friend wasted no time in getting his information passed along. We have an intercept confirming that."

"Excellent news."

"Now… what about our other friend and her contact in Ottawa. Has that happened yet?"

I hesitate for a few moments. From their frowns I see they sense something isn't quite right.

"No, that has not happened. I told her to wait until I had word from you."

"That seems sensible. But, you wanted to meet. What's on your mind?"

"Well, first I have some unsettling news. I assume it is you who warned me of a tail a few nights ago?"

"Yes. Our friends here, Hunter and Gatherer, were the ones who spotted him."

I get it now… they hunt down tails and gather seeds of information. "Yes, well, my tail made an appearance on the evening of the switch."

I can see the alarm spread across their faces, and they glance at Hunter and Gatherer, who seem to be trying very hard not to make eye contact. Clearly, they had not spotted Wilson on that night.

I continue. "Don't worry. He's been eliminated

as a threat."

A collective sigh of relief can be felt if not heard. Intrepid breaks the temporary silence. "Did you know who it was, and have a chance to interrogate him?"

"Yes. I knew him. It was Wilson. What he knew was that Greer and I were both visiting Nadia. That was enough."

"Yes. It was. The silly bastard. Wrong place, wrong time, I suppose. Might I ask, how did you silence him?"

"He's in Rice Lake. Seems that in that snow storm Saturday night he couldn't see where he was going, ran out of road, and inadvertently broke through the ice in his car."

A sombre mood settles over the room. Like me, my handlers aren't enamoured with the more distasteful aspects of our profession.

"Is that all, then?" Finegan asks.

"No. One other thing. It's Nadia. She's been told by her Russian handlers that her mission is coming to a close and that soon she is to catch a train and make her way to the Soviet embassy in Ottawa. She's afraid they will be sending her back home, and who knows what that future will bring."

Intrepid and Finegan both share a look of surprise. Pleasant surprise.

"Is that a problem, Glider?"

"Perhaps. What if they decide she's more of a liability than an asset at this point?"

"And why would they think that? She's completed her mission here, presumably without a hitch. I would say, with the end of the war in site, they'll need her to help consolidate their territorial gains. She's Belarus, right? And speaks Polish, Russian and German, correct? She'd be useful to them… and by extension, useful to us."

I was afraid they would say that. But I don't want to tip my hand at this point.

"I see what you are saying." I leave it at that. I need to think.

"All right… if that's it, then I think we can all get back to our holiday cheer. Good work, Glider… and please tell Nadia to pass along the switched information to her Ottawa contact as soon as possible, and thank her for a job well done. We'll talk about your next assignment in the New Year. And, one more thing… and this time I mean it. Stop using that drop box. You are lucky Wilson didn't take his snooping that far and totally blow your cover. Don't worry, we'll find a new method to get in touch."

I nod, get up and leave. It's time to come up with a plan, and visit Nadia.

On the drive to Newcastle, I turn over various scenarios in my head, the risks coming at us from different angles. I finally think I have a plan that might work, but it's risky and potentially very dangerous. I try desperately to think of something with less risk, but I keep returning to the same idea. It could work. And unless I can miraculously come up with something better, it must work.

I arrive around noon. Nadia seems anxious as she greets me, the strain of not knowing what happens next to her (and us) visibly showing in the furrow of her brow.

"I am glad you came. I need a distraction to keep my mind from wandering. And I need to send those photographs to Ottawa."

We kiss. "I would love to distract you. All day and all night if I could. But, first we need to talk. I have a plan."

"A safe plan, that includes us being together I hope."

"I believe so. Here is what I'm thinking. According to dependable sources, the Nazis have already received their information from Greer. Or at least as much as could travel over wireless. We suspect that once that information is received, a spy within the Third Reich will inform the Soviets of new developments. Think of it as a cross reference to help corroborate the photographs of documents that you send them. Are you with me so far?"

"Yes, I understand. And I believe your suspicions are correct."

"Okay, so, consider this. What if you withhold your film for a time… say ten days to two weeks? What do you think would happen?

"Nothing initially. I suspect though, that at some point they would send someone to investigate me."

"Yes, I think they would. I think they would look at the postmark on your mailing and realize that you had waited to send the information, and then they would send someone to question you."

"Marcus, this sounds dangerous. What would I tell them? Why would I have hesitated to send the information?"

"You won't have to tell them anything. I'll intercept their agent."

"And then what? And how does this help us?"

"I will turn their agent over to my handlers. This will put them in an awkward position with our allies, but it will also mean that, as far as the Soviets are concerned, you've been compromised. We'll have no choice but to keep you here in Canada. Sending you back could mean an interrogation and possible detention, or worse. In short, you would no longer be an asset to either side."

She considers the plan. "I suppose this could work. But, what about the Soviet's attempt to build an atomic bomb? I would still be giving them information, but they will not trust it. Was not the point of this exercise to sabotage their efforts? We will fail in that effort, will we not?"

"In a way, yes, but in another way, no. You see, because they'll believe you've been compromised, they won't be able to trust any of the information you've given them. Meanwhile, they will watch as the Wehrmacht fails in their final attempts, hopefully spectacularly. They won't know what source of information to trust. It won't completely sabotage their bomb-making capabilities, but it will slow them down considerably."

"But one more thing, Marcus. What about your handlers? Will they not also get suspicious of you and me when they determine that I have delayed sending this fraudulent information?"

"That is a risk, yes. I did get the okay today for you to send the photographs. It's ironic that my handler, the master of the double cross, hasn't considered my plan, but he doesn't have the same motivations that we have. That said, I think we're covered. First off, they won't see the post mark, so they won't know when you sent it, unless the operative the Soviets send to check on you tells them and I really don't think that's likely. It's more probable that the operative won't be given specific directives other than to watch you, and to see who you meet with. If he's sent to interrogate you, then that is another story. But he won't get the chance to interrogate you, and he certainly won't tell my handlers why he was sent to interrogate you.

"That reminds me of the other important aspect of the plan. There is another factor at work here too. Have you been reading the newspapers?"

"Yes, of course."

"So, then you know that the Germans launched a counter-offensive on the Western front a couple of weeks ago."

"Yes, through the Ardennes region in Belgium, right? They started on December 16th."

"Yes. And it is failing. They aren't able to break through our lines. The war will be over soon, but not before they take one more shot on the Eastern front. Our intelligence seems to believe that Hitler's generals prefer to lose more ground to the Western allies than to the Soviets. So, I think this means that any of the Germans who are involved in their rocket and atomic bomb development programs will end up in Western hands, not Soviet hands. Bottom line, buying us time not only slows down the Soviet's efforts to build an atomic bomb, it also may help us get those German scientists safely away from the Soviets."

"I see. And I agree. The timing is important, almost as important as the information itself. Oh,

Marcus, you have made me very happy. You have found a way. You have found a way to keep me in Canada and… I hope to keep us together. Please tell me we will be together."

"Yes, of course we will. We just have to be vigilant for the next several weeks."

"Vigilant. And, to be safe, you must spend as much time possible here with me", she says with a shy twinkle in her eye and a brilliant smile.

I'm overcome with a warmth in my heart. In such a short time she has changed me in ways I could not have imagined. Or perhaps she's helped me find a piece of my humanity that I thought I'd lost. Maybe it's being back home, maybe it's trusting and loving someone like Nadia. I feel my time as an agent is going to end soon, because I'm longing to be with her, to live our lives together in the open instead of in the shadows. I must make this plan work, and I must protect her at all costs.

We spend New Year's Eve celebrating together at Nadia's; the champagne is hard to come by but I have enough connections to acquire a half decent bottle of cheap bubbly. We talk of our future, our hopes and dreams. And, we talk of our other dreams too... the ones that keep us awake at night. I'm sad that Nadia is experiencing the same type of anxiety, flashbacks and uneasiness that I've been experiencing, but, that said, talking about it seems to have helped both of us. I find sharing these thoughts as intimate as our love making, and I feel that a bond stronger than ever is forming between us. We talk about everything except the war and Eldorado. The only discussion of handlers is when she asks me to pass the pan handlers, so she can retrieve the pot roast out of the oven. I laugh, and try to explain that the term in English is 'pot holder'… she has a great sense of humour but for some reason doesn't find this particularly funny. And she's right. I love her just a little bit more for that.

Early January passes, with no communication from Intrepid or Nadia's contacts in Ottawa. Nadia and I are together so much that it feels very much like we are a married couple. I spend many nights in her apartment, careful to park my truck some place inconspicuous like the drug store parking lot, and always leaving before sun up the next morning (not difficult as the sun rises as late as 7:50 a.m. at this time of year). And, of course, I have to make sure I avoid times when Greer shows up. Luckily, during the company shut down, he did not come around at all. It appears that his wife and children insisted he vacation with them in Montreal. The few times he has visited, Nadia has feigned sickness and those visits have been cut short. Nonetheless, even the thought of them in the same room makes my skin crawl. Both of us will be relieved when the ruse has ended.

My handlers had insisted that I keep my cover job at Eldorado, despite the fact that the mission is essentially over... perhaps because there are other secrets that Greer might want to pass on, or, maybe they still feel there is value in turning him. Regardless of their reasoning, I've turned into a pseudo husband who often commutes from Newcastle in the early morning to a job in Port Hope. A few times a week I stop at my grandparents' after work for dinner and to drop off groceries and other essentials... we talk of the war, plans for the farm's upcoming season, and local gossip. They have become somewhat suspicious of the mysterious woman I'm spending so much of my time with, however, they don't press me too hard for information. They treat me like the adult that I am, and trust that all will be revealed soon – and I can only pray that they are right.

Nadia has kept the film of the photographed forgeries carefully hidden in the upholstery of her sofa, and in mid-January, we agree that it is time to send it through the post to the post box in Ottawa and ultimately on to the Soviets. This is the point of no return; once sent the date stamp on the envelope will raise a red flag and hopefully send an inquisitive eye from the NKVD.

The German counteroffensive in the forests of Belgium continue to falter, with the American, British, French and Canadian forces having pushed them back to their starting point and beyond. It now seems that we are in a race with the Soviets to see which 'ally' arrives in Berlin first. Some intelligence reports have noted Wehrmacht troops on the move in western Hungary; perhaps this is a sign that the Germans are finally turning their attention back to the Eastern front.

I realize that all of this means much less to me at this point. What matters more than anything else is ensuring Nadia's safety.

Suddenly, in the third week of January, what we had anticipated with both a sense of wistfulness and a small amount of fear, arrives. But not in a way I had ever expected.

It's about four-thirty a.m. and I arise from Nadia's bed to start the day. After showering and getting dressed, I make my daily peek out of Nadia's front living room window through the cobwebs of frost, then return briefly to the bedroom to kiss Nadia goodbye. I don my winter garb, then start the cold trek back to my truck, parked several blocks east.

The ignition turns slowly, as if the truck is as unhappy to leave as I am, but then it relents and finally fires to life. Just then, the passenger door is yanked open and a large man jumps in and points a gun at my face. He's wearing an ill-fitting suit and oversized coat, and a menacing glare. Any lingering thoughts of returning to Nadia's warm bed are quickly erased.

"Let me guess... you are here to deliver a message from Uncle Joe Stalin?"

"Very funny. Now, no more questions. Shut up and drive." His accent confirms my suspicion.

He directs me north out of town, and I do as I'm told. For several minutes, neither of us speak, then he breaks the silence, shoving the gun hard into my rib cage and growling, "So, Mr. Comedian, hand me your wallet. Slowly. I don't want to accidently shoot you in the guts."

Again, I do as I'm told. He takes my wallet and, as he struggles to open it one handed, I entertain the thought of trying to grab his gun. As if reading my thoughts, he pushes the gun harder into my rib cage and scowls at me with malice in his eyes. He jabs the wallet at me.

"Open it and take out your driver license, and all other papers or identifications that have your name on it. And I warn you, when we stop I will look again and if I find so much as a receipt in there with your name on it, you will pay for your stupidity."

Steering the car with my left hand, I take out my driver's license and my last pay statement, silently cursing myself for keeping this piece of paper with me.

"So, you are Marcus Andersen, working at Eldorado in Port Hope. Interesting place to work, no?"

I feel that is a rhetorical question, but since we are now talking, maybe I can use that to my advantage and throw him off balance.

"You have me at a disadvantage, I mean with the gun, yes. But, since we are exchanging pleasantries I would like to know your name and where you work too. I gather from your accent that you aren't from around here."

"Very astute, Mr. Andersen. Let's just call me 'man with gun'. As for my job and where I am from, I think you can guess that too. But that is the last question from you. I am losing patience. Now you will tell me, what do you want with the girl, Nadia?"

"What do I want? Tell me comrade, do you like women? Because if you did, you wouldn't need to ask that question."

My smart-assed reply has the desired effect. The gun is pulled from my chest, but, as he attempts to pistol whip me across the forehead, I duck toward him, plowing my forehead into his face, while grabbing his arm and wrenching it towards the windshield.

The windshield explodes, and, as we wrestle for control of the gun, I slam on the brakes and the truck careens off the road and into a drainage ditch. My assailant and I burst through the windshield, the gun jettisoned from our collective grip, as we stretch out our arms in an attempt to cushion the blow. We land with a thud, both of us too winded to continue the struggle, shocked at the speed of events.

As my blurred vision clears and my breathing starts to return to normal, I look up from the ditch and, to my surprise, see two pairs of heavy black boots. As my eyes scale the heights of these men, I finally focus on their faces, and am relieved to see Hunter and Gatherer, my friends from Twenty Committee.

"Well, Glider, it looks like you found a way to step in the muck again. Who's your friend?"

I glance to my right. My assailant is still alive, but his forehead is badly gashed and he appears to be in shock and likely concussed. He is shaking, his breath raspy and his eyes vacant.

"I've not got his name yet, but it seems Uncle Joe sends his regards."

I see the look of confusion on their faces. They expected a fifth columnist – someone friendly with Adolf and his rabid followers, someone easily disposed of – not a supposed ally. It's also clear to me that with our NKVD friend now knowing both my real name via my wallet contents, and my mission alias 'Glider', via Hunter and Gatherer's greeting, that I am officially compromised... a cardinal sin in the espionage world and one that Hunter and Gatherer have inadvertently played a role in.

Hunter and Gatherer regain their composure, as does the NKVD agent who has likely undergone the same sort of training as all of us spooks. Shock is not an option during a mission. Nevertheless, it appears he's not about to make a fuss, as he's being handcuffed and transported out of the ditch and into the back seat of their warm sedan. Hunter gets in the back seat with him, and I take the passenger seat beside Gatherer who is our driver.

After several minutes, the NKVD agent

speaks. "Reach into my left breast pocket and remove my wallet."

Hunter looks to both me and Gatherer, shrugs his shoulders and does as requested. The NKVD agent speaks again.

"Now, look at the identification in the wallet. What do you see?"

Hunter rifles through the wallet and retrieves a photo ID. "Igor Navikov, military attaché, Soviet embassy to Canada, in Ottawa."

I can't help it. A sardonic smile crosses my lips. Igor looks at me, and despite himself, he also grins.

"Well, well, well. It looks like our friend here, Comrade Navikov, has a get-out-of-jail-free card. Diplomatic immunity."

Hunter and Gatherer ponder this statement I've just made. Gatherer glances at me, and a look of discomfort creases his face. "That may be true. But we'll have a chat with Finegan before we make any decisions."

Igor, on cue responds, "I understand. You are a foot soldier, just doing your job. But, rest assured, none of this officially happened. Now, take me quickly to this Finegan, so we can end all of this unpleasantness."

CHAPTER 18
EXPLANATIONS

As expected, Finegan gets the story out of Navikov. It is not an unpleasant interrogation, given his diplomatic standing. Navikov is short on some details, but his story is nonetheless telling.

Officially, Nadia (aka Sofia Novartov) was doing secretarial and translation work for Navikov and the embassy. He had expected papers from her over two weeks ago, and when they didn't materialize he became worried. He went to check on her and, as he arrived in the early morning hours to begin his surveillance, a man – Andersen – appeared on the scene, exiting Nadia's apartment. Navikov was worried that Andersen might be a fifth columnist, and that he might have compromised Soviet security. So, he followed him to his vehicle and demanded information. His official story beautifully dovetails with the unofficial version.

Navikov ends his story bluntly, "Now, I must insist I call my embassy and tell them all is well. I think we both agree, this episode is best left forgotten."

Finegan agrees, but not before further discussions with Navikov. Discussions that prove just how little I know about counter-espionage.

***

I'm in Intrepid's office, where it all began. He's chagrined with me, and I can't say I blame him. "All right, Glider, what have you got to say for yourself?"

"I suppose I played my hand differently than we had agreed, but, in the end the Soviets are no closer to making a bomb than the Germans are."

"Ah, yes, about that. I forgot to tell you. The Germans had an unfortunate accident. Apparently most of their work to refine uranium was happening at the Kaiser Wilhelm Institute for Physics, located on the edge of the Black Forest near the small town of Hechingen. A week ago our operatives in the vicinity reported that there was a very loud explosion, followed by a fire which consumed most of the institute. No official report yet, but we believe our misinformation found its way into the intended hands and had the desired effect – their refinery has been completely destroyed. So, that at least went to plan.

"Now, Glider, back to you and the debacle

with the Soviets. Why did Nadia hesitate for so long to send that film to her handlers after we gave express permission to send it at the end of December?"

I pause, then knowing that Intrepid will see through any attempt I make to hide the truth, I decide to level with him.

"With all due respect, Intrepid, none of this would have happened without you and Finegan and your future plans for Nadia. You see, I made a promise to her. I told her that she would not be sent back. That she'd be allowed to stay in Canada. But, you threw a monkey wrench into all of that. As soon as I mentioned that the Soviets were recalling her, you couldn't resist planting her as an asset. It's not that I'm naïve. I understand that the ground has shifted… and that our allies will soon be our enemies. But I can't be a part of that, and I can't let Nadia be put in danger. So, I cooked up a plan. A plan that would throw the Soviets off of their bomb making efforts and also put Nadia out of their reach."

I see the look on Intrepid's face as he starts to put the puzzle pieces into place. Thankfully it's not a look of anger or disgust. More of calculation, and perhaps slight amusement.

"So, you told her then to delay passing along the information. You assumed that the Soviets would send someone to check on her; that they would realize that she'd been compromised. You deliberately burned an asset, Glider. You understand that, right? My question is, why?"

I'm about to answer, but I pause. There is something happening with Intrepid.

Intrepid looks at me, the gleam in his eye temporarily gone. It's replaced by a hollow, faraway look. It seems to me that he's reminiscing, thinking of his own life before the war, before all the decisions that he's had to make, which must still weigh heavily on his conscience. He glances down at his desk, then raises his head slowly, his jaw hardened and his eyes back in focus.

"All right, Glider. I think I've kept you in the dark long enough. Tell me, why do you think Hunter and Gatherer were still following you?"

"Well, I assume it's because you or Finegan told them to."

"Yes, but why would we do that? The Germans had already received the falsified documents and, as far as we knew, so had the Russians."

I ponder this. In thinking back, I couldn't imagine that either Hunter or Gatherer had any clue as to the reason they were following me. At the time it hadn't occurred to me to figure out why either; I was just relieved to see them when they showed up. And then it strikes me, with a jolt.

"You were using me as bait. Am I right?"

"Well, when you put it that way it doesn't

sound all that palatable, does it? But, yes, in a sense you were bait, as was Nadia. The plan was hatched when you said that Nadia had delayed sending her information to the Soviets until she had orders from us to do so. I recognized a stalling technique. And, as is so often the case, I thought I'd turn a potential threat into an opportunity."

"So, you knew all along that I was going to compromise Nadia and make her useless to you as a future operative. A bait and switch. You traded Nadia for our new friend Mr. Navikov."

"That is, in essence, what we wanted to do. Although, you made it much more adventurous than we anticipated. Lucky that Navikov wasn't killed by one of you, I suppose. Anyhow, we've persuaded Navikov to work with us now. He will be much more valuable than Nadia given his position as a diplomat. Imagine the misinformation we can send through him?"

Intrepid is now clearly enjoying himself, continuing with his story.

"After Navikov gave us his cover story, which we knew was a lie, Finegan pointed out to him that there were really only two options: one, we could expose him and he'd be sent back disgraced, or, two, we could pretend to fall for his cover story and arrange for some limited success in his continued spying operations here, thus propping up his career. Then at the appropriate time, we would use him to send disinformation, with the promise of extraction and a life of luxury in the west to follow. It was not a hard sell. There are not many agents in the NKVD that trust their boss, that butcher Lavrentiy Beria, and for good reason. The purges carried out by him and Stalin are still very fresh in their collective memories. So now you know. But, despite everything ultimately turning out the way we had wanted, I would still like to know why you decided to go rogue and burn what could have been an important asset?"

It is funny sometimes how the brightest of men can sometimes miss the simplest of things. Something so elementary, so obvious, so incredibly human and yet so incredibly elusive to men who have been preoccupied with war for the last five plus years. I answer Intrepid, and I am, surprisingly even to me, unashamed and unabashed.

"It's simple, sir. I did it for love. I love Nadia. And I love my life here, and the life I hope to have with her. Here at home, in this little part of Ontario where I grew up with my grandparents. Can you see it? My war is over. It started to end the moment I came back to Port Hope and it just picked up steam when I started to fall in love with Nadia. Wilson was the last straw. I can't do it anymore, sir, and I don't want her to have to do it anymore either. Fortunately for me, Nadia feels the same way."

Intrepid looks at me, his face a mask. I don't know if he's going to call in guards to take me to a holding cell, or hug me. Then as he gives a tight nod I see that his mind is made up.

"Very well, Glider. I can't make you serve if you no longer want to. This is not a 'till death do us part' type of assignment. And, at any rate, you've been compromised as much as Nadia has. I suppose in the end I can't find fault with your logic, especially since it so conveniently fit with our goals. Every mission objective has been accomplished and, as a bonus, our hero ends up with the girl. Glider, you are dismissed."

"Yes, sir." I nod, salute, and make my way towards the door. I'm interrupted.

"And Gilder… one more thing. Officially, Nadia is dead. Apparently, after Finegan talked to Navikov, he decided that it would be best to tell his bosses that he had to eliminate her. Her name is now Nora Olsen. A nice Norwegian girl that I'm sure your grandparents will approve of. You can get her passport and other papers on the way out. Good luck and all the best, Marcus. We thank you for your service."

I'm left speechless. Intrepid smiles, then gets back to shuffling papers around his desk, trying desperately to avoid eye contact. I leave quietly, hardly believing what has just happened.

I feel light as a feather as I make my way to the truck. I leave in a hurry, catching a last glimpse of Camp X in the rear view mirror. The drive to Newcastle takes less than half an hour. Nadia… Nora! … is waiting at the door. She's a vision, dressed in her Sunday best. She skips down the steps of her apartment and pecks me on the cheek as I hold the truck's passenger door open for her.

"How did it go?" She asks as she grabs my hand.

"Better than I could have dreamed. We're free, Nadia. We are out of it."

Her smile lights up the interior of the Ford. She nestles her head on my shoulder and we both enjoy the silent thoughts running through our minds. Then she looks up at me, a slight frown creasing her forehead.

I read her thoughts. "Don't worry. They are going to love you. How could they not?"

"They could judge me. I've corrupted their grandson."

"Nonsense. They have been looking forward to this day for weeks now. They could tell I'm in love, and when they meet you they will know why. They're happy for me."

We drive in silence for a while, enjoying the sunlight on this cold winter day, the wind swirling snow against the shoreline of Lake Ontario, blowing and glittering. Nadia shifts her weight off my shoulder and looks at me with concern etched across her face; a stark contrast to the serene winter views.

"Marcus, you must know… it's not just your

grandparents that worry me. I have a past; one that overlaps with yours. How can I be in Port Hope knowing that he's there? How can I ever walk down the street knowing that he could suddenly appear out of the blue? If I see his fat face and his pig eyes I could go mad. I don't know what I'd do…"

I don't know whether she's going to pound the dashboard in frustration or simply slump over in her car seat and cry. She's a mishmash of pent up emotion. I'd meant to tell her later, when we were alone, after she had been through the rigours of meeting my grandparents, but clearly I have miscalculated. It's time to tell her.

"Nadia, Greer won't be a problem."

"How can you say that? Of course he's a problem. For both of us."

"I'm sorry. I was going to tell you later. I thought meeting my grandparents today would be enough to deal with. Greer will be incarcerated for a very long time. Intrepid has already called in the RCMP and he'll be picked up this afternoon and held incognito until a trial, charged under the Official Secrets Act. He's of no use to us now even if we thought we could turn him."

She ponders this news. I can see she's conflicted.

"What's the matter?"

"I feel sorry for his wife and kids, that's all. Will I be asked to testify?"

Her comment about Greer's family is a reminder to me. A reminder that I've lost something that I'm trying desperately to get back. A reminder of why I've fallen so hard for this woman, who despite everything still has the capacity to empathise.

"No, you won't be testifying. A sworn testimony with your name redacted will be adequate. Besides, Greer will crack and confess when he's confronted with the evidence: his bank statements, documentary evidence in his house and car, the intercepted messages from the Swedish embassy. He's in so deep there will be no climbing out. Of course, the fact that you were passing information to the Soviets won't be revealed. Everyone has agreed to that, and that the trial will remain secret so you are not exposed. As for his wife, I'm told that Greer wasn't the only one stepping out on their marriage. With the divorce settlement, she and the kids should be fine."

She's looking at me now, and appears to be mapping out something in her head. Some dots are still not connecting.

"But, am I not just as guilty of spying? I don't understand this."

"Nadia, this was my plan, remember? And our Soviet friend Igor played right along in his 'official' interrogation. As far as anybody but a handful of people know, you were never a spy. You're an immigrant… a poet trying to scratch out a meagre existence in your new country. You were doing freelance secretarial and translation work for the Soviet consulate in Toronto. As for Greer, you met him and had an affair, and yes, you did see some interesting documents in his possession. End of story."

She seems satisfied with this answer, but I can see another question forming.

"So, I just live my life as Nadia Mironov? How can I do that, after all that has happened? Won't the Soviets come for me again? They have ears. They will know my testimony is only partially true."

I reach in to my breast pocket and pull out the documentation.

"They might look for Nadia Mironov, but they won't find her because she doesn't exist anymore, because Navikov had to eliminate her. You are now a nice Norwegian Canadian girl named Nora Olsen. I'm sure my grandparents will approve."

The clouds of dismay disappear from her eyes. A smile plays at the corners of her mouth. Her shoulders relax and she regains her position, lying against my shoulder.

"Nora Olsen," she whispers, "I like it."
I've never seen her so content, and by extension, I

feel content myself. The war will end soon and I'm back home, in love with a strong, independent, beautiful woman.

    Perhaps with time both of us will be able to put the war behind us. I know talking to her about my experiences and hearing her talk about hers have already helped both of us. I no longer find myself having 'flashbacks' interrupt my days. My nightmare of being suffocated and burned in my hideout has been happening with much less frequency, and when it does, I have her to comfort me and bring me back to the here and now. And, the here and now is good. Very good

AUTHOR'S NOTES

This is a work of historical fiction. I stress the word fiction. So, for those of you interested in something more historical I will set the record straight.

First off, as with my first book, the story is centered in and around what is now Northumberland County and Durham Region, in southern Ontario, Canada. The story of Eldorado (now known as Cameco) and its role in the herculean effort carried out by the allies – principally the Americans – to develop an atomic bomb is an interesting one. Numerous volumes have been written about it. An excellent brief can be found on-line:

https://nuclearsafety.gc.ca/eng/resources/fact-sheets/Canadas-contribution-to-nuclear-weapons-development.cfm

To summarize this article: Eldorado played an important role in the refining of radium (mined in the Northwest Territories and shipped to Port Hope) to extract uranium, however, this uranium was not weapons grade. For that, further processing was required. That was done in the United States.

The production of weapons grade uranium for the Manhattan Project, as the story notes, is done by a process called thermal diffusion. If one reads up on the Manhattan Project, there is mention of an accident at a refinery in Philadelphia where the pressure built up during this process caused an explosion, killing several servicemen. I've used this unfortunate event, but, in my story, the specifics of the faulty process are used in a counter espionage exercise designed to sabotage Nazi efforts to produce an atomic bomb.

Which brings us to this question: Were the Nazis ever close to making an atomic bomb? Most experts agree that they were not. I refer the reader to an excellent write-up online:

https://en.wikipedia.org/wiki/German_nuclear_weapons_program

The short answer is that the Germans were familiar with nuclear fusion as early as 1939 but by 1942 had largely given up the thought of weaponizing it as impractical. That said, many of the scientists that had worked in the Third Reich were 'recruited' to work for the Soviets after the war and contributed to their development of an atomic bomb, first tested successfully in 1949. By then, the cold war was in full flight, with former allies jockeying and eyeing each other suspiciously across Europe and, eventually globally. The book shows glimmers of the bourgeoning cold war.

As for the Soviets spying on the British, American and Canadian scientists involved in the Manhattan Project, again, I refer the reader to this excellent article in Wikipedia:

https://en.wikipedia.org/wiki/Soviet_atomic_bomb_project#Espionage

Historians agree that the Soviet program benefited from Communist sympathizers that had access to information as early as 1942, including men like British physicist Klaus Fuchs and the American Theodore Hall, a theoretical physicist.

This brings us to the crux of the story: espionage, and it's closely related cousin, counter-espionage.

One of the more fascinating figures of World War II is the Canadian spy master Sir William Stephenson, referred to in my book by his code name 'Intrepid'. At the outset, before Americans officially joined the allied war effort, Stephenson worked tirelessly to set up a spy network that included American co-operation. In addition to this, he also set up "Camp X" near Oshawa, Ontario, Canada to train men and women from Britain, Canada, the US and Nazi-occupied countries in counter-espionage.

These operatives, once trained, worked domestically in both Canada and the United States to thwart any fifth columnist activities. Foreign agents would be secreted behind enemy lines to coordinate with underground resistance movements and generally wreak havoc. The opening paragraphs of this book outlines one such episode that happened: the destruction of the Vemork power station and the plant there that produced heavy water, at the Rjukan waterfalls in Norway.

To read more of the exploits of this Canadian hero, I'd recommend the book '*A Man Called Intrepid*' by William Stevenson. There are also numerous books and online resources outlining the history of Camp X.

Intrepid is the only main character in this book based on an actual person and his role during the war. That said, I couldn't help but name drop a famous son from Port Hope as a minor character. Vincent Massey (the first Canadian born Governor General of Canada) plays a bit role in my fiction. His Batterwood estate remains a jewel located just outside of the town of Port Hope. C.D. Howe is also mentioned. He was, as advertised, the Canadian wartime industrial czar. Everyone else was conjured from my imagination.

As with my first book, the locales are all very real. Locally, visitors to the area can travel all the roads mentioned, many of them very scenic, and, if they wish, drive their car directly into Rice Lake at the Gore's Landing boat launch. Also, during the war there was a part of Toronto referred to as 'Little Norway' which was populated by expat Norwegians, many of whom would enlist to fight the Nazis who had overrun their homeland. A plaque is all that remains of this community.

Manufactured by Amazon.ca
Bolton, ON